WORLD HISTORY

The Ancient World
40,000 – 500 BC

Kingfisher an imprint of Larousse plc
Elsley House, 24-30 Great Titchfield Street, London W1P 7AD

This edition published 1997
This edition Copyright © Larousse plc 1997
First published by Kingfisher 1992 as *The Kingfisher Illustrated History of the World*
Copyright © Larousse plc 1992, 1995

British Library Cataloguing-in-Publication Data
A catalogue record for this book is available from the British Library

ISBN 07534 0127 4

Typeset by Tradespools Ltd, Frome, Somerset
Printed in Italy

Contents

What is History?

The word 'history' comes from the ancient Greek *histo*, 'know this'. In Greek 'I know' also meant 'I have seen', and *historeo* came to mean 'learn by inquiry'. The Greeks thought that you cannot know anything unless you have either seen it for yourself, or made an inquiry about it. The Greek historian Thucydides wrote that far too many people were willing to believe the first story that they heard!

The ancient Greeks understood the essence of what history is. First, historical knowledge must be based on evidence ('that which has been seen'). Second, history is not one story, but several. And third, that everything must be checked for errors. Historians try to find out not only what happened but why it happened.

The word 'history' has many meanings. It is an account of past events, in sequence of time; it is the study of events, their causes and results; and it is all that is preserved or remembered about the past. For evidence historians use written

▲ *Buildings tell us a lot about the past. The Romans erected huge public buildings and many, such as the Colosseum, Rome, still stand.*

◄ *Events in modern history are often well documented such as the meeting of the 'Big Three' war leaders, Churchill, Roosevelt and Stalin, at Yalta after World War II.*

accounts, artefacts such as weapons and tools and oral (spoken) accounts. To remember something people write it down, or commemorate it in some way. This is because events, even important ones, quickly disappear from memory. Our lives may seem very different from the past, but some things have not changed; Roman roads are still used every day and games like chess were played centuries ago.

The Work of Archaeologists

Archaeology is the study of people of the past by the scientific analysis of the things these people left behind. Archaeologists study objects (artefacts), features (buildings), and ecofacts (seeds or animal bones). Archaeology can tell us about societies which existed before written records were made, as well as adding to our knowledge of literate societies.

Archaeologists are like detectives. They treat the things they find as clues to the lives of the people who used them. Like historians, archaeologists can sometimes discover the reasons for great changes in the societies they are studying. Kathleen Kenyon, digging at the site of ancient Jericho in 1952, found out that its famous walls were destroyed in biblical times, not by resounding trumpets but by fire!

Archaeology can often present historians with evidence that makes them re-examine their views of early societies. In 1939 at Sutton Hoo in England, the remains of an Anglo-Saxon treasure ship were discovered. The artefacts found there show a far from primitive society of the so called 'Dark Ages'.

Since the 1950s, archaeologists have been concerned with finding general theories that

▲ *Undersea archaeologists carefully plot the position of artefacts aboard a shipwreck. The silt on the sea bed often preserves objects in a remarkable condition.*

▼ *It is very important that the exact position, size and condition of finds is recorded. Great care is taken in excavating to prevent damage.*

▶ *A grid is used to locate and record finds. All earth removed from a site is collected in buckets and later sifted in case any small find has been missed.*

Awning

◀ *Accurate written records are taken. At each level the site is also photographed. This gives a find an exact position.*

Coloured poles to judge distances and height

WHEN IT HAPPENED

1748 Excavations of town of Pompei begin.
1799 The Rosetta Stone is discovered, Egypt.
1870 Heinrich Schliemann begins excavating site of Troy in what is now Turkey.
1879 Prehistoric cave paintings are found in Spain.
1900 Sir Arthur Evans begins excavating Knossos, Crete.
1922 Howard Carter discovers Tutankhamun's tomb, Egypt.
1925 Flint points found at Folsom, New Mexico.
1939 Sutton Hoo treasure ship is found, England.
1952 Kathleen Kenyon excavates Jericho, Jordan.
1970 'Tollund Man' is discovered, Denmark.
1974 Tomb of Shi Huangdi is found in China.
1991 A diver discovers cave paintings in France; 5000-year-old body found in the Alps.

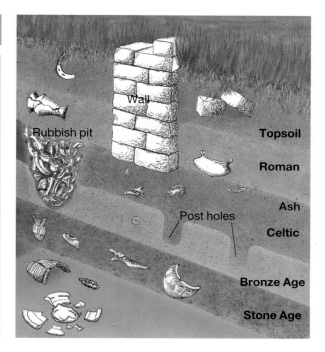

explain the changes that occur in human societies. They now try to find out why farming developed in Mexico around 7000 BC or why the first cities grew up in the Near East. Archaeologists also study specific problems not just sites. In the 1960s Richard MacNeish studied cave sites in Mexico to document making bread from corn. Computers are used to process the statistics and have made this sort of study much faster and more efficient.

▲ A site's history is revealed in layers. The post holes show that a Celtic stockade on this site was replaced by a stone wall during Roman times. An ash layer indicates that the site burnt down.

SCHLIEMANN

Heinrich Schliemann (1822–1890) excavated Troy, the city of Homer's *Iliad*. The site in Turkey had nine cities built, one on top of the other. Homer's Troy was probably the sixth city.

◄ The body of a Danish woman buried in AD 95. Her body was preserved from decay by being in a peat bog.

3

Buildings often reveal clues about how people lived in the past. Stonehenge in England is linked with the phases of the Sun and Moon and archaeologists believe it is an ancient calculator or computer, used to find the best times for planting and harvesting, two important times of year.

Artefacts, such as coins, pottery, tools, weapons and ships are sometimes found in great abundance. Their study can add to our knowledge of social and military history. Ecofacts (often found near artefacts), such as animal bones, skins and plant seeds, help identify the jobs people did and what they had to eat.

Pictures can provide valuable information. We

► *In the centuries before photography paintings are the only enduring record of what people looked like. This wall painting from the Roman town of Herculaneum in Italy shows a mother watching her daughter's music lesson.*

▼ *Aerial photography can sometimes help archaeologists where books, maps and documents may not provide clues. Crop-marks seen from the air show the outlines of Roman forts or Celtic settlements. This picture shows a Roman street plan.*

► *Wooden objects can be dated using dendrochronology, or tree ring dating. Tree growth is affected by the weather and this can be seen in its rings. Over a period of years a pattern develops in the rings. Known patterns can be traced in wooden objects up to 8000 years old to date them.*

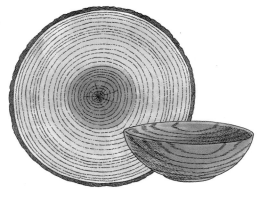

CARTER

In 1922 Howard Carter, (1874–1939) working with the Earl of Carnarvon, found the fabulously rich tomb of Tutankhamun, who ruled Egypt from 1333–1323 BC. The discovery of the tomb was one of the most sensational moments in the history of archaeology.

◄ *Radiocarbon dating is used to date specimens up to 60,000 years old. All living things constantly absorb carbon-12 and carbon-14. Carbon-14 is unstable and, after death, decays, so decreasing the ratio of carbon-14 to carbon-12. Using a particle accelerator, scientists measure the amount of carbon-14 to carbon-12. The lower the ratio, the older the object is.*

can tell a lot about what people looked like and what they did before photography was invented from cave paintings, frescoes, portraits and pictures in stained glass. Pictures can also tell the story of a society. The Bayeux Tapestry (which is really an embroidery) tells the story, in pictures and words, of the Norman invasion of England in 1066. It also tells a less well-known story – that of Harold Godwinsson being shipwrecked off the coast of France and his encounter with Duke William, his future rival.

▼ *We know a lot about the lives of ancient people because of their belief in life after death. The tombs of rich Egyptians were filled with things that would make the afterlife more comfortable. They made models of their servants; the ones below show a servant making beer and the crew of a ship.*

The Work of Historians

Before the age of writing, history was passed on by word of mouth (the oral tradition) from generation to generation. The Vikings told *sagas*, or stories, many of which have now been confirmed as fact. Long before Columbus, Leif Ericsson sailed to North America and named it Vinland. Many ancient stories were written down a long time after they happened. Homer's *Iliad*, the story of the siege of Troy around 1250 BC, was probably written down centuries after it happened. No one can be sure how true the story is, but the site of Troy has been found.

The oral tradition forms the history of many African and Aborigine people and can be found in many poems and songs. These tell of migrations, power struggles and battles as dramatic as any that happened in the Europe of ancient times.

Some events recorded in the Bible are now thought to have really happened. For example the area known as Mesopotamia lay between two rivers and was prone to flooding. This was probably the origin of the story of Noah's Ark.

The first real historian was Herodotus. He used the Greek word *historia* to mean 'investigation'. Although Herodotus was writing at a time when everyone believed their lives were controlled by the gods, he also looked for rational explanations and was the first person to look at the causes and effects of events.

Sometimes history is written by those who play a major part in it. Julius Caesar (100–44 BC) wrote about the wars in Gaul (France) and, according to his own account, was merciful to the defeated Gauls. He granted them Roman

◄ The Rosetta Stone, found by Napoleon's invading army in Egypt, was the key to deciphering Egyptian hieroglyphic writing.

PARKMAN

Francis Parkman (1823–1893) wrote *The Oregon Trail* about his life with Sioux Indians. His multi-volume work *France and England in North America* includes the role played by Native Americans in the struggle for power in North America.

RANKE

Leopold von Ranke (1795–1886) wrote histories of 16th and 17th century France and England and of Germany and Prussia. He also wrote a history of the world up to the time of Otto I, the Holy Roman emperor, who died in AD 973.

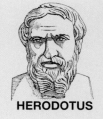

HERODOTUS

Called 'the father of history', Herodotus (c.485–425 BC) set out to write a true and systematic record, based on evidence. He wrote about the Greek and Persian wars and the Pyramids of Egypt.

citizenship as a way of establishing order. Caesar may have written his history to show his actions were not just done for personal glory.

Diaries are a valuable source for historians. John White accompanied the 1584 expedition to establish the first English colony in America. He brought back to England his writings and drawings about the daily life of Native Americans. His records are first-hand accounts of events which would otherwise have been lost, because the rest of the colony perished.

Not all historians witness the events they write about. Most depend on accounts and documents produced at the time. Those who write history must always be aware of bias or prejudice in themselves and in

other writers. Bias means being influenced by a particular point of view and prejudice literally means 'judging before' – before all of the facts have been looked at. Historians must also avoid the mistake of writing about the past as if all events

▼ *The Dead Sea scrolls include the oldest known biblical manuscripts and may have been written at the time of Christ.*

▲ *A 19th century print showing the American Declaration of Independence in 1776. It set out the idea that all people have rights.*

were leading with a fixed purpose to the present. The events in Eastern Europe and the former Soviet Union between 1989 and 1991 show that change can be sudden, and that trends, thought to be fixed, can be reversed.

Local History

Oral history is a good source of local history. Listening to older people's recollections, looking at their photographs and sharing their memories reveal a lot about life in the past. They may have objects or mementos that they kept from their early lives or that have been passed on to them by their parents or grandparents.

were often recorded in the front of a family Bible. When women married in the past, they usually changed their names; this meant every generation of married women would introduce a new family name. It is unusual for one family to be based in just one place for any length of time and many people who study family history try to find out the reasons why members of their families moved to other places. Was it a job, a sweetheart, or some other reason, such as war or religious and even racial persecution?

diaries, letters, census returns, old photographs, records of large estates (in towns and the country), school log books, and business accounts from firms which have long since ceased to trade. Parish records give details of baptisms, marriages and funerals. Families that have had a connection with one place stretching back

▲ Letters, diaries, menus and bills can give us a vivid picture about everyday life in the past.

▶ An old family photograph taken in 1909 showing two generations of the same family.

Family history is a branch of local history. Photographs of family members may reach as far back as great-grandparents or even great-great-grandparents. Important family events

Local record offices store

a very long time (over 1,000 years) may find a reference to their family in the *Domesday Book*, compiled in 1086 by order of William the Conqueror. No survey of the British Isles was conducted again until 1801.

The Ancient World

When this period of history begins the world was still in the grip of the last Ice Age. Vast ice caps and huge glaciers covered northern Europe, Asia and North America. Further south, however, in what is now Africa, the Sahara was green and fertile. While people in the north shivered in caves, hippopotamuses splashed around in the warm waters of the Sahara.

The earliest humans learned how to use fire to keep themselves warm, cook food and scare away wild animals. From being hunters and gatherers of wild fruit, berries and seeds, they slowly found out how to grow crops and keep animals. Eventually they settled down to build houses, villages and the first cities.

The first civilizations began on the banks of river systems where the land was extremely fertile: the Euphrates and Tigris in what is now Iraq; the Nile in Egypt; and the Huang He or Yellow River in China. For a time another ancient people flourished on the banks of the River Indus in present-day Pakistan, and a little later advanced civilizations grew up in the Americas.

Many of the greatest inventions, such as the wheel and writing, occurred during this period, but with events that happened before the invention of writing, archaeologists can only give approximate dates. Later in the period, historians often disagree about the exact dates of events. Nevertheless it is fascinating to compare what happened in different places at about the same time.

For example, while Pharaoh Cheops (Khufu) was urging his workers to finish the Great Pyramid in Egypt, ancient Britons were building Stonehenge in England; farmers in Peru were growing cotton at the same time as the people of the kingdom of Kush in Africa were learning to work metal; and only a few years after the first Olympic games were held in Greece, Chinese astronomers first observed an eclipse of the Sun.

▼ *A village on the River Nile, Egypt in about 3000 BC. The early Egyptians used papyrus reeds not only for their huts but also to build boats.*

NOTE: Most dates in the period before Christ (BC) are approximate.

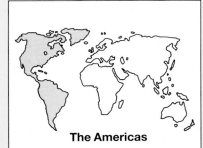

The Americas

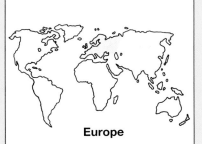

Europe

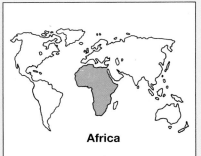

Africa

The Americas	Europe	Africa
35,000 First Americans cross from Asia.	**40,000** Cro-Magnons enter Europe from the Near East.	
25,000 People live in caves in Brazil.	**30,000** Neanderthals disappear.	**30,000** Neanderthals die out.
	25,000 Cave art flourishes in Spain and France.	**15,000** Last rainy period in northern Africa.
		6000 Early rock paintings.
5000 Corn (maize) cultivated in Mexico.	**5000** Land bridge between England and France disappears.	**5000** Civilizations develop in Fayoum and Nubia.
3500 Potatoes grown in South America.		
3372 First date in Mayan calendar.		**2920** Menes rules a united Upper and Lower Egypt.
3000 Agriculture develops in Mexico; coastal towns built in Peru.	**3000** Windmill Hill culture in England.	**3000** Lake Chad drying up, Sahara becoming a desert.
		2630 Step Pyramid in Egypt.
	2700 Building of Stonehenge, England begins.	
	2500 Skara Brae in Scotland destroyed.	**2551** Great Pyramid begun.
2000 Cotton grown in Peru.	**2000** Minoan Crete dominates the Mediterranean.	**2000** Bantu begin migrating south from Central Africa.
	1900 Mycenaean culture in Greece develops.	**1640** Hyksos usurp Egyptian throne.
	1450 Thera (Santorini) volcano erupts, Greece.	**1550** New Kingdom in Egypt. People from Palestine settle there.
1500 Stone temples built in Mexico.	**1400** Knossos, Crete, destroyed.	
	1100 Dorians invade Greece.	
1200 Olmec civilization develops in Mexico.	**900** Etruscans flourish in Italy.	*c.* **1270** Israelites leave Egypt.
	814 Foundation of Carthage.	**1179** Sea People attack Egypt.
850 Chavín culture appears in Peru.	**776** First Olympic games.	**1140** First Phoenician colony in Africa at Utica.
	753 Foundation of Rome.	**1070** End of Egypt's New Kingdom.
	700 Homer's the *Iliad*.	**750** Kush conquers Egypt.
	621 First written laws in Athens.	
	539 Greeks defeat the Carthaginians.	
	510 Last king of Rome deposed, republic formed.	

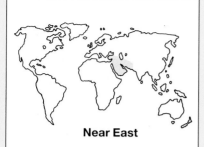

Near East

Asia and the Far East

Australasia and Pacific

10,000 Beginnings of agriculture.
6000 Çatal Hüyük in Anatolia flourishing.

3760 Bronze in use.
3200 Sumerians invent cuneiform writing.

3000 Wheeled vehicles in use.

2300 Semites invade Mesopotamia.
c. **2100** Abraham leaves Ur.
1950 End of the empire of Ur.
1595 Hittites conquer Babylon.

1300 Medes and Persians move into Iran.
1116 Assyrians conquer Babylon.
922 Israel splits into Israel and Judah.
612 End of Assyrian empire.

550 Cyrus the Great founds the Persian empire.
525 Persia conquers Egypt.

18,000 First carved rock reliefs crafted.

4000 Yang Shao period in China.
3500 Copper in use in Thailand.

2697 'Yellow Emperor' in China.
2690 Indus Valley civilization.

2200 Jomon culture in Japan.
2150 Aryans begin invasion of Indus Valley.

1500 End of Indus Valley civilization. Shang dynasty in China.

1200 Aryans in India.
1122 Zhou dynasty in China.
1000 *Rig Veda* compiled in India.
800 Development of India's caste system.
722 Period of loose confederations in China.
563 Birth of the Buddha.
551 Birth of Confucius.

30,000 First people reach Australia.

4000 Colonization of the Pacific islands begins.

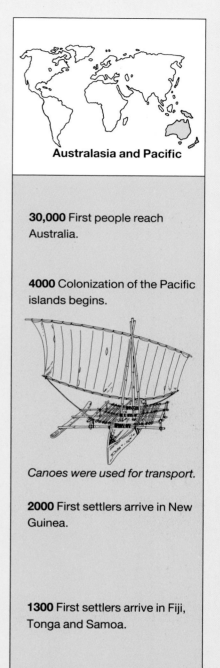

Canoes were used for transport.

2000 First settlers arrive in New Guinea.

1300 First settlers arrive in Fiji, Tonga and Samoa.

The Ice Age

Changes in the Earth's orbit around the Sun may cause ice ages. When they occur, the climate at the North and South Poles becomes extremely cold. Ice caps form, and spread south and north from the Poles. Life becomes impossible under the ice, and difficult near it. The climate of the whole world changes.

The Ice Age was at its height around 16,000 BC. This was the most recent of a series of ice ages that have occurred over the last 2300 million years. It is the one that most affected humans.

During the Ice Age, the Arctic ice cap spread south to cover northern Europe and Asia, the whole of Canada and the Great Lakes area of the United States. With so much water locked up in ice, the sea level fell by about 90 metres.

As a result, there was dry land between northern Asia and Alaska, between Australia and New Guinea and many Indonesian islands. The British Isles and Europe were linked by land that covered the southern part of the North Sea. The Thames was a tributary of the Rhine.

▲ *During the Ice Age people were limited in the areas where they could live, but they managed to exist in caves on the edges of the ice. In the caves they left wall paintings as a record of the animals they knew. In this re-created scene ibex are being pursued by huntsmen armed with spear-throwers.*

▶ *The Leakey family – Louis, Mary and their son Richard – spent many years looking for fossils of early humans in Africa. Here Mary Leakey is examining foot prints of a human-type creature that are about 2.5 million years old. It was warm in Africa while ice covered most of Europe.*

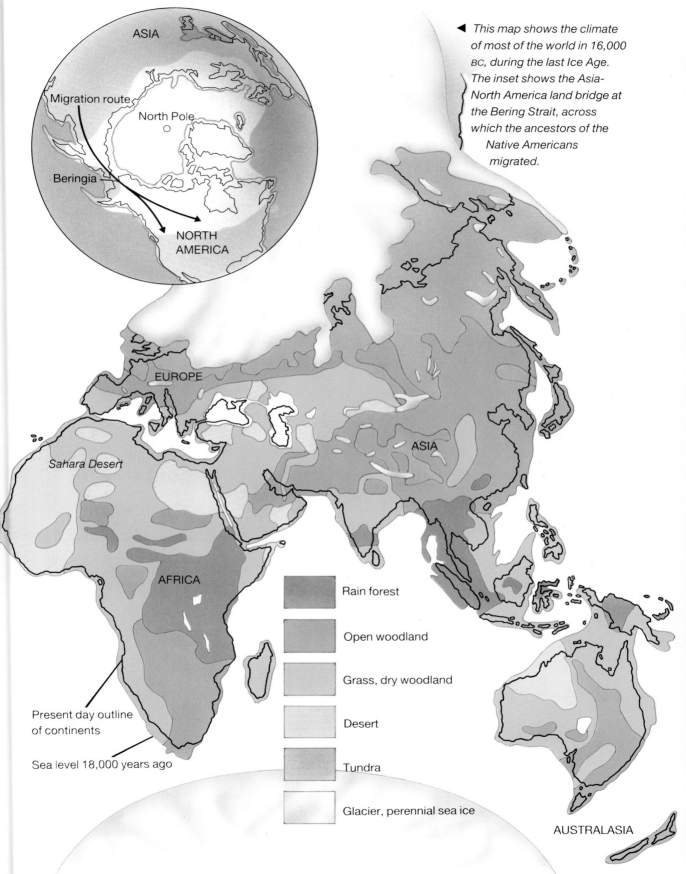

◀ *This map shows the climate of most of the world in 16,000 BC, during the last Ice Age. The inset shows the Asia-North America land bridge at the Bering Strait, across which the ancestors of the Native Americans migrated.*

ASIA

Migration route

North Pole

Beringia

NORTH AMERICA

EUROPE

ASIA

Sahara Desert

AFRICA

Rain forest

Open woodland

Grass, dry woodland

Desert

Tundra

Glacier, perennial sea ice

Present day outline of continents

Sea level 18,000 years ago

AUSTRALASIA

The First People

The earliest hominids, or human-like creatures, are called Australopithicines. Many of their bones have been found in Africa. They walked upright and made simple tools from pebbles. They were probably not true humans because their brains seem to be very small.

The earliest species of true humans, belonging to the genus *Homo* (human), first appeared about two million years ago. Called *Homo habilis* (handy human), they lived alongside the last of the Australopithicines.

The most advanced of these early humans is known as *Homo erectus* (upright human) and their remains have been found in Africa and Asia. By learning to use fire, this species was able

▲ *The first people made fire by using a bow to spin a stick against another piece of wood.*

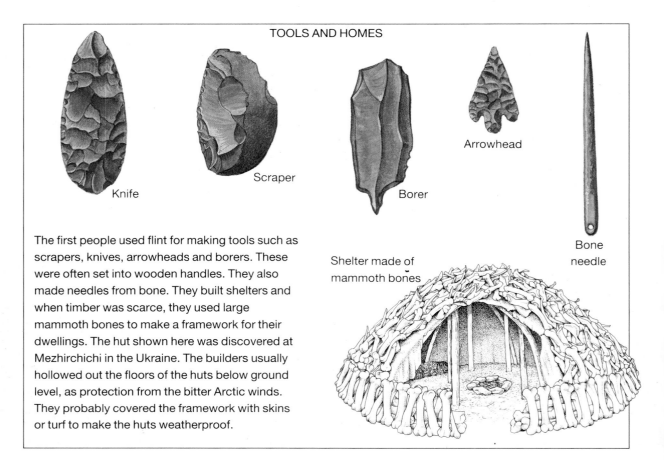

TOOLS AND HOMES

Knife

Scraper

Borer

Arrowhead

Bone needle

The first people used flint for making tools such as scrapers, knives, arrowheads and borers. These were often set into wooden handles. They also made needles from bone. They built shelters and when timber was scarce, they used large mammoth bones to make a framework for their dwellings. The hut shown here was discovered at Mezhirchichi in the Ukraine. The builders usually hollowed out the floors of the huts below ground level, as protection from the bitter Arctic winds. They probably covered the framework with skins or turf to make the huts weatherproof.

Shelter made of mammoth bones

PIGMENTS

The first people used many natural pigments (paints) to decorate their bodies and their homes. In Europe, Cro-Magnons painted the animals they hunted using black, yellow, red and white pigments. More than a hundred decorated caves have been found in Europe and many rock paintings exist in Africa and Australia.

EARTH MOTHER

One of the earliest statues known is called the Venus of Willendorf, named after the place in Austria where it was found. It was probably carved between 25,000 and 15,000 years ago. Archaeologists think it represented a god-dess, probably the Earth Mother.

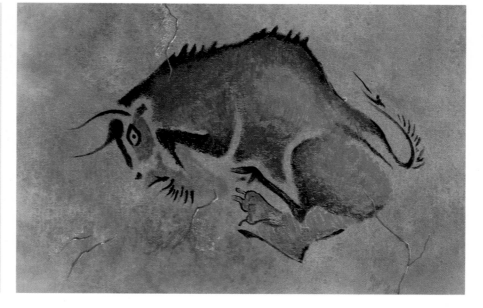

to move into icy Europe, cook and keep warm, and drive away wild animals. Next followed *Homo sapiens* (wise human), which flourished from about 200,000 years ago. One type, called the Neanderthals, were particularly adapted to living in a cold climate and were able to survive in northern Europe. They developed many types of stone tools.

The humans who live today are probably descended from the Cro-Magnons who seem to have entered Europe from the Near East and replaced or mixed with the Neanderthals. The first people lived by gathering fruits, berries and roots and hunting wild animals.

▲ *Early artists painted animals, like this bison, deep inside caves.*

▼ *An encampment of hunters in eastern Europe about 25,000 years ago. Hunting in groups, they could kill very large animals such as the mammoth. The hide was used for clothing and shelter and the meat and bones were cooked in large pit fires.*

Arts and Crafts

The mammoth hunters who lived in Europe over 25,000 years ago made little clay models of women and of animals. No one knows whether these were just works of art or whether they were religious. Later hunters painted pictures of animals deep inside caves. Once people started leading more settled lives, they had more time to make pottery and other items. In China the people of Yang Shao painted pots with geometrical patterns on them. As bronze replaced stone for weapons and tools, metalworkers became important craftsmen. They made objects which were not only practical, but beautiful. As towns and cities grew, temples and important buildings were decorated with carvings and paintings.

▲ *The Cro-Magnons made realistic models of animals, like this bison which is carved from an antler.*

▼ *This Olmec figure is carved in jade. It represents a jaguar spirit, associated with Tlaloc, the god of rain and fertility.*

▲ *This delicately-carved ivory head found in France may be the world's earliest known portrait. It was carved over 24,000 years ago.*

▲ *This fish from the Egyptian New Kingdom is a bottle for cosmetics. It was made from strips of coloured glass wrapped round a core. The ripples were made by drawing a point across the glass before it hardened.*

WHEN IT HAPPENED

c. 27,000 BC Mammoth hunters in Europe make clay figures of women and animals.

c. 25,000 BC Hunters paint animals on the walls of the caves at Lascaux in France.

c. 6000 BC People at Çatal Hüyük, Turkey, have necklaces made from shells.

c. 3500 BC At Yang Shao, China, pottery painted with geometric patterns is made.

1323 BC Tutankhamun is buried in Egypt.

c. 1200 BC The Olmecs, Mexico, carve huge human heads out of basalt.

▶ *Houses and palaces in Mycenae in Greece were decorated with frescoes like this. A fresco is a picture painted on wall plaster while it is still damp. This one shows a boar hunt.*

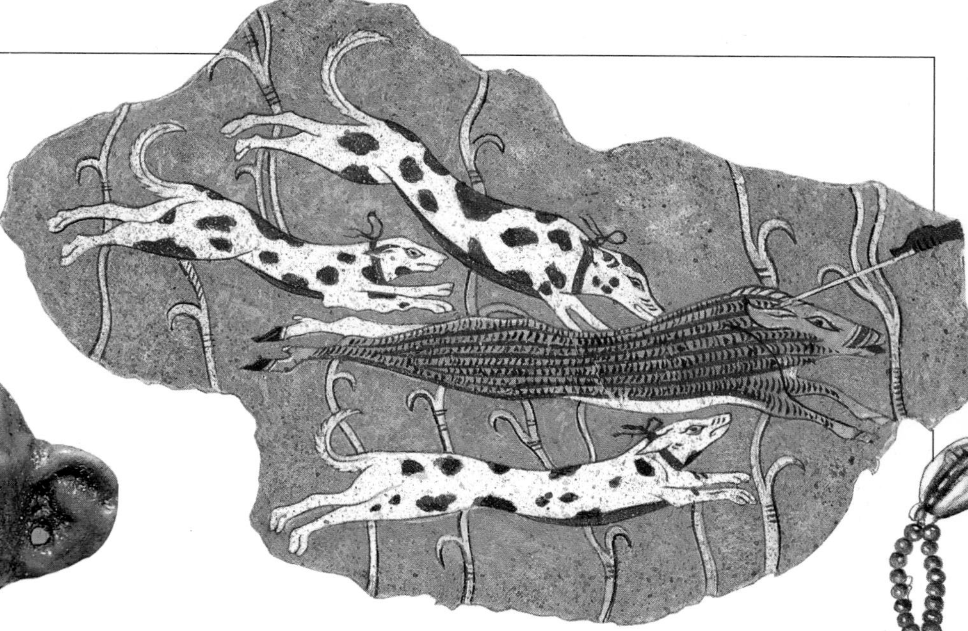

◀ *The Egyptians liked to have statues of their pets. This monkey is made from glazed earthenware.*

▲ *This necklace from the Egyptian Middle Kingdom has silver cowrie shells with beads of amethyst, lapis-lazuli, carnelian and feldspar. Hanging from it are charms shaped like fishes, beards and lotus flowers.*

▶ *The Sumerians believed they should always serve the gods. When they could not pray in person they left stone statues of themselves to pray for them. This man was a government official called Ebih-il.*

BC

40,000 Last Ice Age: Cro-Magnon people, the first modern humans, begin to enter Europe from the Near East.

35,000 Around this time humans cross the Bering Strait land bridge to America from north-eastern Asia.

30,000 First humans reach Australia from southern Asia, partly by land bridges, partly by boat. Neanderthal people seem to disappear in Africa and Europe after existing for about 70,000 years. Hunters roam southern Europe.

A spear-thrower lengthened the hunter's throwing arm and meant that he could throw his spear further. This was probably the first machine ever invented.

25,000–20,000 Cave art flourishes in southern Europe, especially at Lascaux, France and Altamira, Spain. Figurines of Great Mother-Goddess, made of stone and ivory in Europe, found in Nile mud in Egypt. People in south-east Asia use rafts. Early cave settlement, with wall decoration, flourishes in north-eastern Brazil.

18,000 Earliest known human sculpture made in Asia.

15,000–10,000 Africa cooler than today – last rainy period in northern Africa.

10,000 End of the last Ice Age. Hunting weapons develop. Disappearance of large mammals in North America. Humans reach the tip of South America.

10,000–9000 Beginnings of agriculture in the Near East and eastern Asia. Ceremonial burials of bodies coated in red ochre in Czechoslovakia and Iraq, associated with goddess worship.

The First Farmers

People's lives changed with the development of agriculture. Slowly people discovered that certain plants could be grown or cultivated to provide crops and certain animals could be protected or domesticated (tamed) to provide meat, milk, hides or wool. Gradually many people began to rely on the steady supply of food from their crops and animals and instead of moving from place to place to gather their food, they started to settle in fertile areas of land.

Farming and civilizations grew up in several parts of the world, including China, Africa and Central America. Some of the earliest farmers settled nearly 10,000 years ago in what is often called the 'Fertile Crescent'. This was an area of land which was watered by the Tigris, Euphrates and Nile rivers. Here people grew wild wheat and wild barley, and

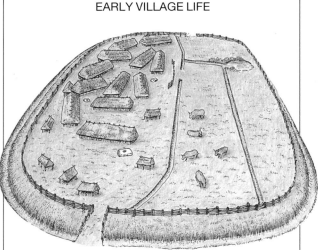

EARLY VILLAGE LIFE

An aerial view of a European farming village about 4500 BC. The large enclosure contains shelter for cattle and pigs. Peas, beans and lentils grew in vegetable patches in front of the houses. Villages of up to 50 dwellings are known to have existed. In time, the crops and grazing animals exhausted the soil and the people had to move to new sites.

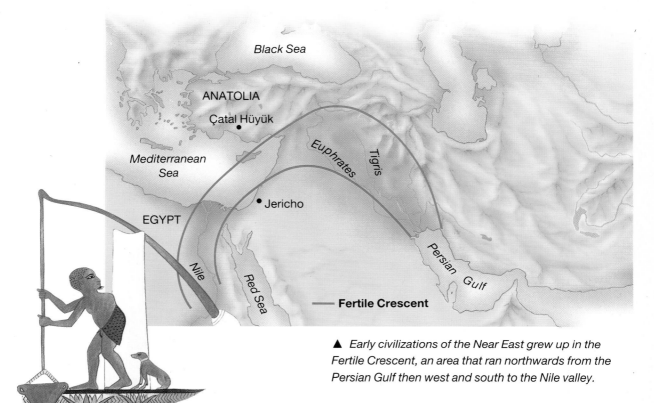

▲ Early civilizations of the Near East grew up in the Fertile Crescent, an area that ran northwards from the Persian Gulf then west and south to the Nile valley.

◄ A shaduf is used to raise water for irrigation. A weight on one end of the pole balances the water-filled leather bucket on the other end.

kept goats, sheep, pigs and cattle.

The first animal to be domesticated was the dog, and it is likely that dogs adopted humans just as much as humans began to keep dogs. This probably began as far back as 10,000 BC. Dogs were used to herd other wild animals, who in turn were domesticated. Soon breeding began to change the animals.

One of the most important inventions for agriculture was irrigation, a system of supplying cultivated land with water. Farmers in the Fertile Crescent and America dug out channels to carry water from the river to their crops. Using reservoirs and sluice gates, land lying far from the river could be made fertile.

After many generations these farming settlements grew and established the first cities and civilizations.

CROPS

The early farmers harvested wild wheat and barley. They then sowed some seeds to raise new crops. Farming grew rapidly when wild wheat crossed naturally with a kind of grass. It produced a new form of wheat with plump seeds. People were able to cultivate this wheat and use it to make a new form of food: bread. Farmers used simple tools such as hoes and crude ploughs. They reaped the crops with sickles made of flint.

Wheat

Barley

Buildings

The earliest humans lived in caves or any other natural shelter they could find. The first buildings they made were like tents of animal skins supported on wooden poles. In places where wood was scarce, they used mammoth bones for supports. Eventually they started making more comfortable homes for themselves. Many of these were made of mud and wood and so they have long since rotted away. Luckily archaeologists have been able to find enough evidence to show us what some of these houses were like and how they were built. However, not all buildings were made for people to live in. Some were made for religious purposes and others were made as tombs for the dead. Often these were built from stone and so they have survived to the present day. They include the pyramids and temples in Egypt, and Stonehenge in England.

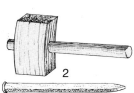

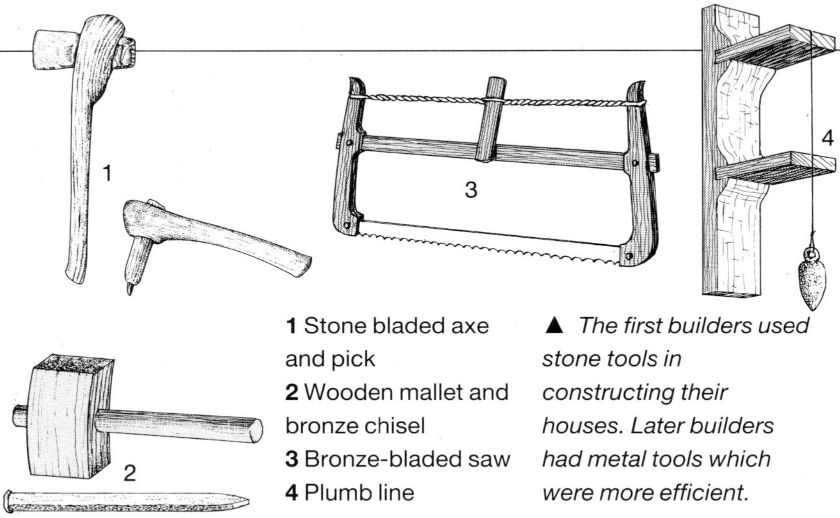

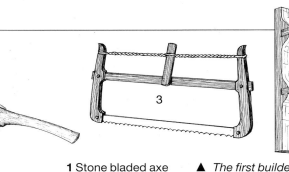

1 Stone bladed axe and pick
2 Wooden mallet and bronze chisel
3 Bronze-bladed saw
4 Plumb line

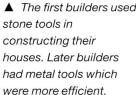

▲ The first builders used stone tools in constructing their houses. Later builders had metal tools which were more efficient.

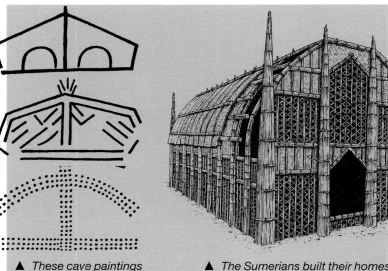

▲ These cave paintings may show plans for huts.

▲ The Sumerians built their homes out of marsh reeds.

▼ The pyramids were built on the edge of the desert with a causeway connecting them to the River Nile. The funeral procession landed by boat and then went along the causeway to the mortuary temple where the funeral was performed. The body was then buried in the pyramid. The pyramid was seen as a ramp to the sky.

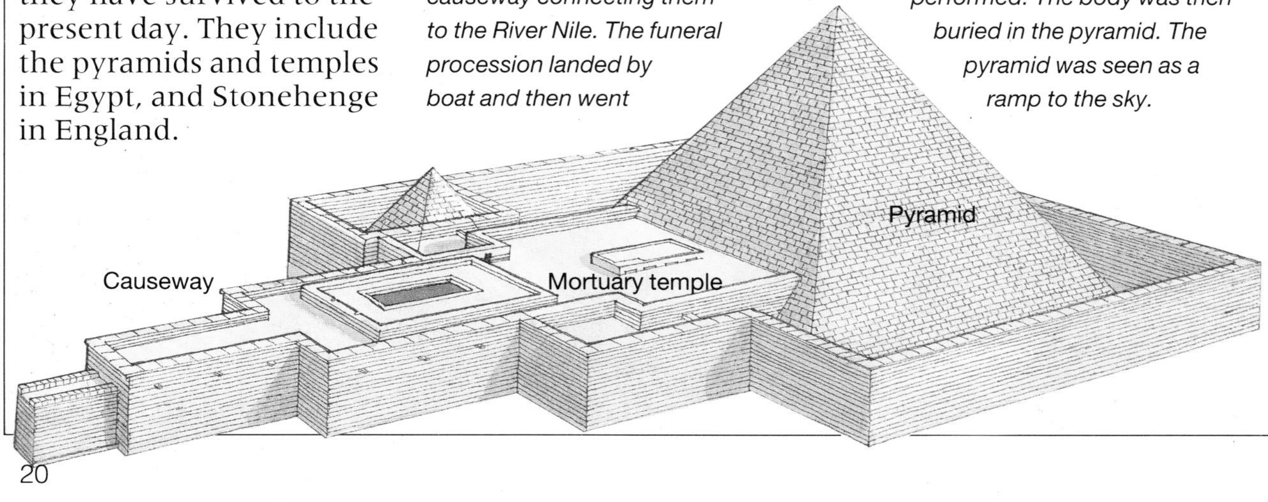

Causeway

Mortuary temple

Pyramid

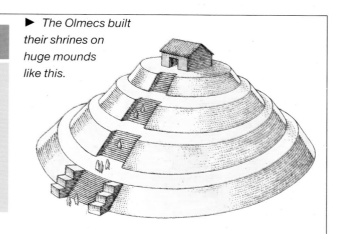

► The Olmecs built their shrines on huge mounds like this.

▼ Egyptian temples had many stone pillars carved to represent the papyrus plant and the palm tree.

◄ Houses in Jerusalem had flat roofs. Each one had to have a parapet, or low wall, to stop visitors falling over the edge.

Open papyrus

Palm

Bundle papyrus

▼ In Europe the first farmers made their house walls of hurdles of woven twigs, plastered with clay to keep out the wind and rain.

The First Cities

One of the oldest cities known is Jericho which lay on the west bank of the River Jordan. The battle of Jericho, which is described in the Bible as when the walls came tumbling down, was fought about 3500 years ago. But the ruins of some of the city's walls are 11,000 years old. They were massive structures of stone, and some may have been as high as 7 metres.

The walls of ancient Jericho were rebuilt at least 16 times. They were probably destroyed not by a series of battles, but by earthquakes. Inside the city walls, the houses and other buildings were built from mud bricks and had flat timber roofs.

Çatal Hüyük is another ancient city. Its ruins are in Anatolia, Turkey. It may well have been as ancient as Jericho, but

THE EARLY USE OF POTTERY

Pottery developed at about the same time as agriculture because pots were needed to store grain and to hold water. This pot was discovered near Çatal Hüyük and it is nearly 8000 years old. It was decorated to resemble plaited reeds. At first people made pots out of clay dried in the sun, like their mud bricks. They soon found that baking the clay in a fire made it much harder and longer lasting. Pottery of advanced craftsmanship and decoration was made both in the Near East and in the Yang Shao settlements of China.

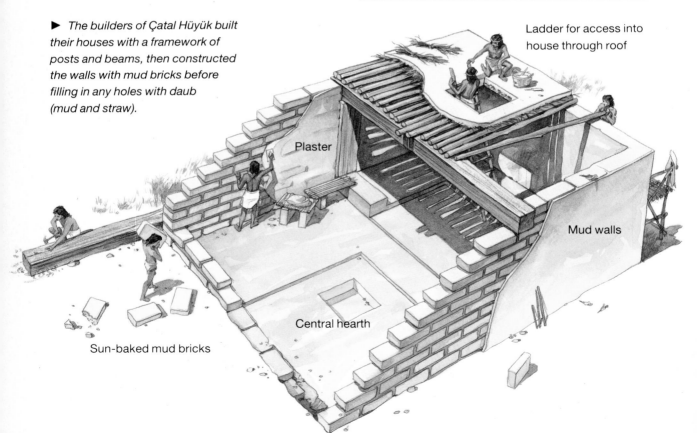

▶ The builders of Çatal Hüyük built their houses with a framework of posts and beams, then constructed the walls with mud bricks before filling in any holes with daub (mud and straw).

Ladder for access into house through roof

Plaster

Mud walls

Central hearth

Sun-baked mud bricks

▲ *A model of a Chinese house from about 2000 BC. The roof was held up by wooden posts. Remains of posts have been found where the Yang Shao lived.*

▼ *The houses in Çatal Hüyük were so tightly packed that there were no streets. People had to walk along the rooftops, then use ladders to enter their homes. This also meant it was difficult for enemies to get in.*

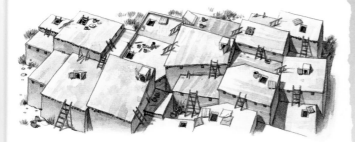

the earliest ruins we know of date from about 6250 BC. By then about 6000 people lived in Çatal Hüyük in mud-brick houses. They covered the walls inside their houses with fine plaster, on which they painted decorations in a red pigment. Some of their furniture was made, like the walls, from mud bricks.

While cities were growing up in western Asia, other settlements were rising in the east, in what is now China. The Yang Shao people, who lived in a fertile river valley between the Huang He and its tributary the Wei He, built a number of small, self-contained villages.

BC

9000 Near East: Sheep, goats, cattle and pigs are domesticated; development of Middle Stone Age culture. Earliest walled settlement built at Jericho. Americas: Arrowheads of this date found at Folsom in North America.

8400 Americas: First known dog was kept in the Idaho Valley.

8000 Europe: Spread of agriculture to Europe. Near East and Eastern Asia: Copper is in use. Anatolia: Early settled villages in eastern part of the region. North America: Humans hunt bison. Japan: Pottery is being made.

7600 About this time the Irish Sea and then the Strait of Dover begin to open up as the sea level rises, gradually separating Ireland from Great Britain, and Great Britain from Europe.

The first bricks were made of mud and left to harden in the Sun.

7000 Near East: The city of Jericho continues to flourish despite repeated destruction. First shrines to the Mother Goddess erected there. Pottery develops. The use of brick for building begins in the Near East.

6000 Near East and Europe: The Neolithic (New Stone Age) period begins. Anatolia (modern Turkey): The settlement at Çatal Hüyük is already flourishing and contains 6000 people. Shrines to the Mother Goddess are set up there.

6000–5000 Near East: The earliest known use of looms for weaving at this time. Crete: The earliest settlements are established. There is trading in obsidian and flint.

North Africa: Early rock paintings are made in the Sahara region.

BC

5000 Africa: New Stone Age people work polished stone. Development of civilizations begins at Fayoum and Nubia in the Nile river valley. Agriculture begins to spread southward. China: Yang Shao people establish village farm communities along the banks of the Huang He. Mesopotamia: Sumerians establish their first agricultural settlements in the river valleys of the Tigris and Euphrates. Europe: As the ice cap continues to melt, the rising sea level severs the last land bridge between Great Britain and mainland Europe. Mexico: People begin cultivating corn (maize). Australia: Hunters are using the boomerang to bring down animals for food.

4500 Sumer and Egypt: Real metal work begins, heating and pouring metal into moulds.

4000 China: Yang Shao farmers cultivate rice.

A drawing of an alabaster vase found in the temple at Uruk. It shows the fruits of the harvest being given to a priestess.

4000–3500 Sumer: First towns are founded including Ur and Uruk (Eridu). The potter's wheel is first used. Disastrous floods hit the region, probably giving rise to the biblical story of Noah's Ark. Coloured pottery from Russia reaches China. Egypt: White painted pottery is produced. Crete: Ships sail in the Mediterranean Sea.

Mesopotamia and Sumer

The first people to settle in Mesopotamia were the Sumerians who arrived there more than 7000 years ago. Their civilization consisted of a number of city-states or cities that were also independent nations.

Each city-state had fine public buildings, a water supply and drainage. It had a royal palace for its ruler and a *ziggurat* or tower, on top of which was a temple dedicated to the god that the city worshipped. Around the public buildings were the houses of the people. Beyond them lay the fields of the farmers. Further out were the marshlands for which southern Mesopotamia was noted.

The Sumerians devised the first known writing system. From about 3200 BC they wrote on clay tablets. Thousands of these tablets have survived, containing accounts and letters revealing that as

▼ *Mesopotamia lay between the Tigris and Euphrates rivers. Its name came from the Greek for 'between the rivers'. Some of its more powerful city-states, shown on the map, conquered their neighbours.*

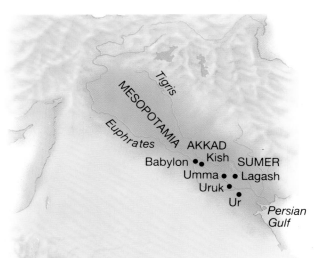

SARGON OF AKKAD

Sargon of Akkad founded a Sumerian empire in 2360 BC. From his city-state of Akkad he conquered other Sumerian cities. His empire reached as far north as Syria.

▲ *A reconstruction of the ziggurat at Ur. On the top was the temple, where the king (who was also the high priest) performed religious rites and sacrifices. The ziggurat was built of sun-baked clay bricks.*

well as textbooks and history, the public services were well developed. Royal graves have also been found containing treasures that show the Sumerians' wealth and the skill of their craftsmen.

Many Sumerian traditions have been passed on to us today. Their ancient poem *The Epic of Gilgamesh* describes a flood which is very similar to the biblical story of Noah's Ark (*see* pages 44–45).

The rulers of one city-state called Ur extended their lands to form an empire, which included Babylon. The Babylonian language was spoken throughout Ur.

THE WHEEL

No one knows when the wheel was invented. The first wheel was probably the potter's wheel, used to make perfectly round vessels. Carts like this were certainly in use in Sumer more than 5000 years ago. An important weapon of war developed from the cart: the chariot. Warriors from the north in chariots later overwhelmed Sumer. The wheel was also used as a pulley to lift heavy loads.

▼ *The Sumerians of Mesopotamia built and lived in reed houses on the southern marshlands. This picture of twentieth century Marsh Arabs on the banks of the Tigris in southern Iraq shows that tradition lived on.*

Ancient Egypt

The civilization of the whole of ancient Egypt depended on the River Nile, which flooded every year, depositing rich silt (soil) along its banks. With this, the Egyptians were able to cultivate a long, narrow strip of land on either side of the river. Here the workers grew wheat and barley to make bread and beer, and flax for linen with which they made most of their clothes. They reared cattle mainly as beasts of burden.

For most of their history, the ancient Egyptians were united under one ruler. At the top was the *pharaoh* (king). He was worshipped as a god. The Egyptians believed in an afterlife, so they developed the custom of embalming (preserving) the bodies of the dead. They also built elaborate tombs for them and decorated them with paintings and inscriptions in Egyptian picture-writing or hieroglyphic ('sacred writing') script.

In between the pharaohs and workers were officials who ran the government, priests who served in temples and merchants who traded.

UPPER AND LOWER EGYPT

The small communities along the River Nile became two large states in the 4th millennium BC. Lower Egypt occupied the Nile delta and Upper Egypt ran south from the delta for about 800 km. In about 2920, Menes, king of Upper Egypt became the ruler of both states after they were united. The pharaohs of Egypt are generally grouped in dynasties (families). The most important periods are the Old Kingdom (2575–2134 BC), the 4th to the 8th dynasties; the Middle Kingdom (2040–1640BC), the 11th to the 14th dynasties; and the New Kingdom (1550–1070 BC), the 18th to the 20th dynasties. Many of the Pyramids and the Sphinx at Giza were built during the Old Kingdom.

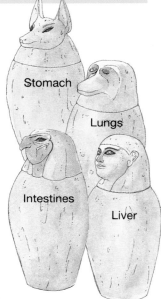

► A group of funeral urns, known as canopic jars, were used to contain the vital organs taken from a body before it was embalmed. The lids show the heads of four minor Egyptian gods called the Sons of Horus, represented as a jackal, a baboon, a hawk and a man. They were often made from stone, wood or pottery.

Stomach

Lungs

Intestines

Liver

◄ Ploughing the fields with a pair of oxen, as shown in a tomb painting from about 1300 BC. The annual flooding of the River Nile kept the land very fertile.

► The white crown stood for Upper Egypt and the red crown, Lower Egypt. After the two lands were united the pharaohs wore a double crown.

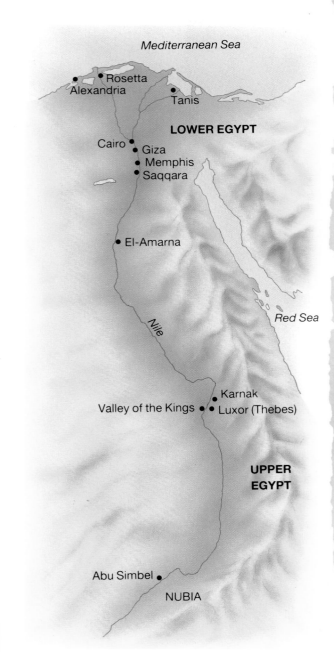

▲ *Important places in Egypt throughout its early history.*

BC

3800 Sumer: Earliest known map, inscribed on a clay tablet, it shows the River Euphrates.

3760 Earliest date in the Hebrew calendar, for long the traditional date of the Creation. Egypt and Sumer: Early use of bronze is recorded.

3500 Near East: Flax is being grown for making linen; irrigation canals are dug in Mesopotamia. Egypt: Two kingdoms of Upper Egypt and Lower Egypt flourish side by side. The earliest known numerals and a hieroglyphic script are invented. Development of the mastaba, a burial pit covered by a brick platform. South-East Asia: Copper tools come into use in what is now Thailand. South America: farmers grow potatoes.

3372 North America: First date in the Mayan calendar.

A mastaba was a platform built over a burial pit and was the forerunner of the pyramid. Mastabas were also the tombs of noblemen.

The first pyramid was built at Saqqara and is called a step pyramid because of its shape.

The shape of the true pyramids of Giza developed from earlier forms. They were the largest of all and the most carefully built.

27

Communications

Once people started trading with each other, they had to find ways of keeping a record of the goods they bought and sold. One way of doing this was by writing the information down. The earliest writing to be discovered so far dates from around 3200 BC and comes from Mesopotamia. Here the Sumerians drew tiny pictures on clay tablets. These were probably records and accounts of traders. Over the next 200 years these pictures were replaced by wedge-shaped patterns made with a chopped off reed. Each pattern represented a sound or a syllable. This sort of writing is called cuneiform. The Egyptians knew about it, but they invented a writing system of their own, called hieroglyphics. They wrote on sheets of papyrus, made from the papyrus reed. These were lighter and more convenient than clay tablets. In China the earliest surviving examples of writing are from the Shang dynasty. Over 2000 different characters have been found on oracle bones from this time, suggesting that writing was already well developed.

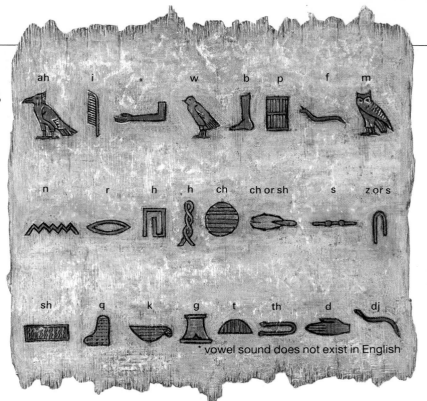

* vowel sound does not exist in English

▲ The early Egyptian hieroglyphs each represented a different object. Later ones stood for sounds, rather than things.

► Egyptian scribes used a holder for their brushes and a palette for their ink.

▼ Scribes were important people in Egypt. Their training took up to twelve years. They became civil servants, teachers or librarians.

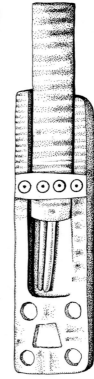

Brush holder

Palette

► *Mycenaean writing, found on baked clay tablets at the palace of Knossos in Crete. This script is called Linear B. The tablets tell us what was in the palace storeroom, such as weapons and chariot wheels. This writing probably developed into the modern Greek alphabet.*

► *This map shows where four of the earliest known forms of writing developed. They were all based on pictures which were later simplified.*

Cuneiform

Chinese characters

Egyptian hieroglyphs

Indus Valley glyphs

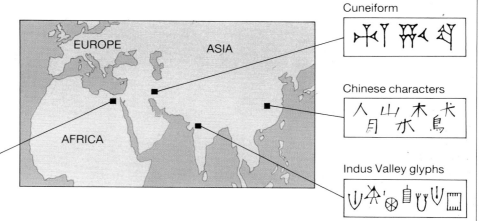

► *There was more than one Chinese language, but everyone who could read could understand Chinese writing. This was because each symbol stood for an object, not a sound.*

WHEN IT HAPPENED

c. 3200 BC Sumerians begin to develop cuneiform writing, the oldest known writing system.

c. 2600 BC Papyrus used in Egypt. Before this, the Egyptians wrote on stone.

c. 2000 BC Basis for the modern alphabet appears in the eastern Mediterranean countries.

c. 1500 BC Chinese writing appears on oracle bones, but Chinese have probably been using writing since c. 2800 BC.

c. 1400 BC Mycenaeans use the script called Linear B for their palace records.

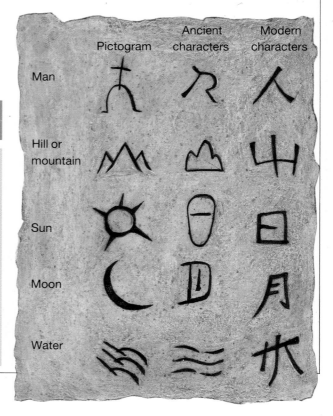

	Pictogram	Ancient characters	Modern characters
Man			
Hill or mountain			
Sun			
Moon			
Water			

Megalithic Europe

All around the coast of western Europe are ancient Stone Age monuments built of megaliths, which means 'huge stones'. The most impressive of these monuments is Stonehenge, in southern England. It was built in three stages from 2750 BC onward, forming a circle of huge, dressed (shaped), upright stones linked by lintels (beams). Scientists think that it was used as a temple and a place to study the stars.

Even older than Stonehenge is the Avebury stone circle, a few miles to the north. It is a much larger ring of stones which have not been shaped.

Stone circles are found elsewhere in the British Isles. One example is the Ring of Brodgar in the Orkney Islands, off north-eastern Scotland, which is about the same age as Stonehenge. The stones there are all tall, thin and pointed.

At Carnac in Brittany, north-western

▲ Skara Brae, in the Orkney Islands, was a Stone Age village that was buried by sand at the height of a fierce storm 4500 years ago. The people fled, leaving pottery, bone pins, stone tools and even a necklace behind.

▼ Stonehenge on Salisbury Plain, England, is one of the most elaborate megalithic monuments in Europe. Its layout was arranged to mark the midsummer sunrise and the midwinter moonrise. To erect the largest stones the people must have used ramps, ropes and levers. The huge blocks of stone were dragged many kilometres using only wooden rollers.

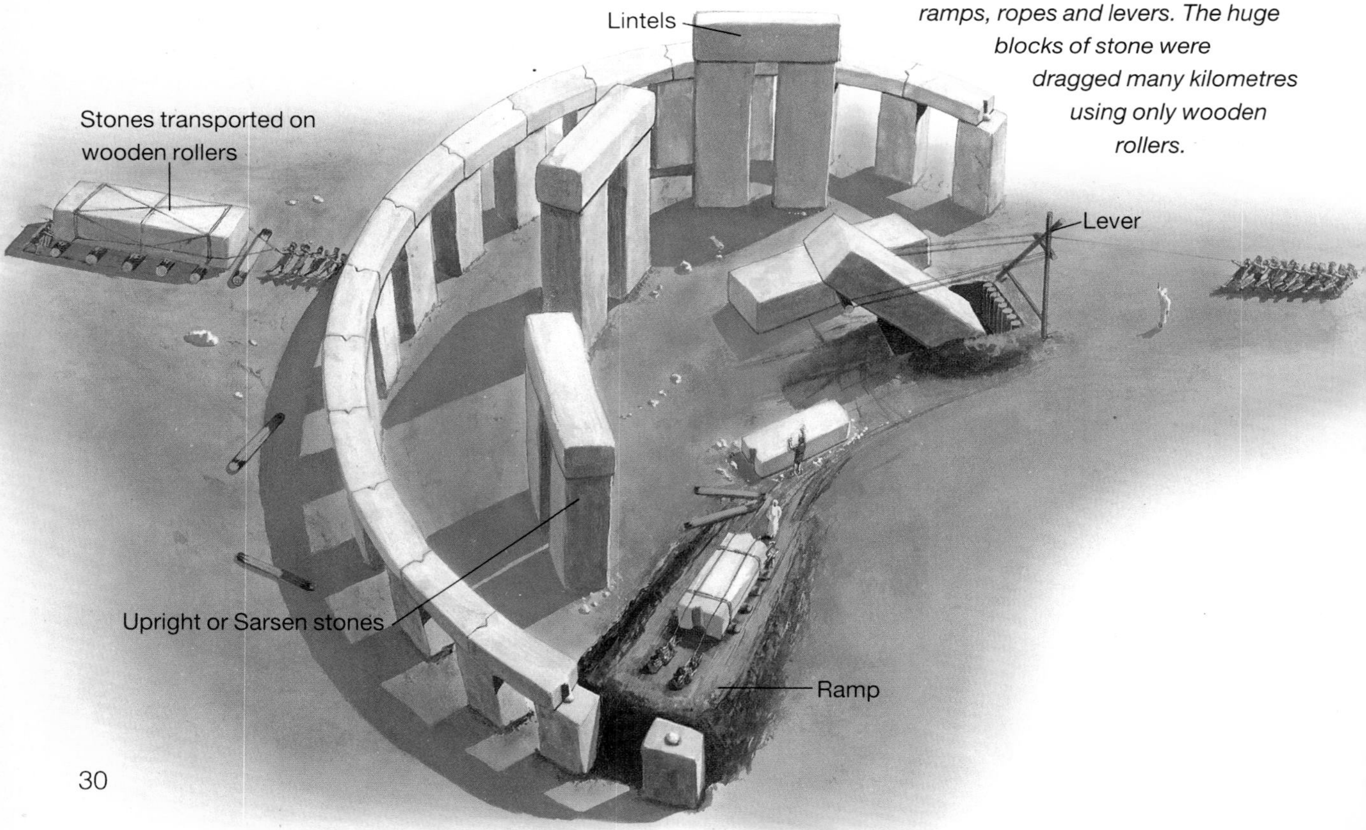

Lintels

Stones transported on wooden rollers

Lever

Upright or Sarsen stones

Ramp

France, there is a series of avenues of standing stones, stretching for several kilometres and erected in the New Stone Age. Brittany also has many single standing stones, called menhirs.

Many barrows or stone-built graves covered with soil and turf are found in France and England. In some cases the soil has been removed, leaving standing stones with flat slabs resting across them.

Another remarkable collection of megalithic monuments is in Malta and its sister island of Gozo. Some of the oldest have walls made of huge stones 6 metres or more long and 3.5 metres tall. Several of the temples, such as those at Hagar Qim and Tarxien, contain dressed stones carved with simple designs. The most remarkable Maltese monument is the Hypogeum, an underground temple carved on three levels deep into the rock.

RELIGIOUS BELIEFS

We can only guess at the religious beliefs of Stone Age people. Undoubtedly stone monuments, like this one at Carnac in Brittany, France, had a great significance, possibly as meeting places for worship and sacrifice.

Stonehenge, and some other circles, were positioned either to help with observations of the heavens, or as vast outdoor calendars. They suggest some form of Sun worship was practised.

Some of the stone temples contain altars. The Hypogeum on Malta has an 'oracle hole', which magnified the voice of a priest or soothsayer.

BC
3200 Sumerians devise first known system of writing, using 2000 pictographic signs inscribed with a stylus on clay tablets. The script appears in an inscription on the temple at Uruk of the Mother Goddess, under her title Queen of Heaven. Sumerian farmers grow barley, and make wine and beer. Scotland: First houses are built at the village of Skara Brae, in Orkney.

3000 Ukraine: Wild horses are domesticated. England: Settlers at Windmill Hill, Wiltshire make pottery; Avebury stone circle in Wiltshire is begun, and also nearby Silbury Hill. Phoenicia: Settlers occupy the eastern Mediterranean coast. Iran: The Elamite civilization flourishes. Africa: Lake Chad begins to dry up and the Sahara begins to form as a desert. Mexico: Development of agriculture in the Tehuacan Valley. People make their first pottery. Peru: Villages and towns are built on the coast. Anatolia: Troy flourishes as a city-state. Bronze Age begins. Crete: Stone villages are built. Trade flourishes with Egypt, the Levant and Anatolia. Mesopotamia: The first iron objects are made; Sumerians first use wheels on vehicles. Europe: Weaving loom introduced from the Near East.

2920 Egypt: Pharaoh Menes unites the kingdoms of Upper and Lower Egypt, founding the first dynasty.

A tomb in Portugal, built using giant stones (megaliths). Tombs like this have been found all over western Europe dating from 4000 BC.

31

The Indus Valley

The early peoples of the Indian sub-continent lived around the Ganges and Indus rivers. The first civilization sprang up in the Indus Valley, now in Pakistan. The two largest cities in the valley were Mohenjo-daro (which lay about 320 kilometres north-east of Karachi) and Harappa (which was some 200 kilometres south-west of Lahore). At the centre of both Mohenjo-daro and Harappa lay an artificial mound, which served as a citadel (stronghold). On this mound stood a large well-aired granary. Beyond the citadel were shops and the workers' houses.

Each house was built around a courtyard, and had several rooms, a toilet and a well. All the buildings were built of bricks, baked in wood-fired ovens. The citadel at Mohenjo-daro even had a bathhouse, with private baths round the outside of a much larger public one.

Among other crops, the farmers of the

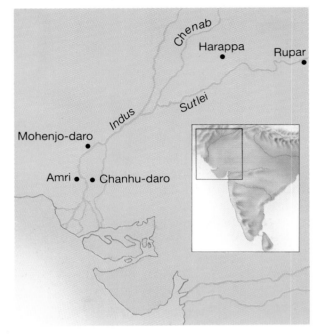

▲ The main places of the Indus Valley civilization. It flourished at a time when the climate of the region was much wetter than it is today.

▼ An artist's impression of Mohenjo-daro as it may have looked at the height of its prosperity. This city was built on a grid pattern like modern American cities.

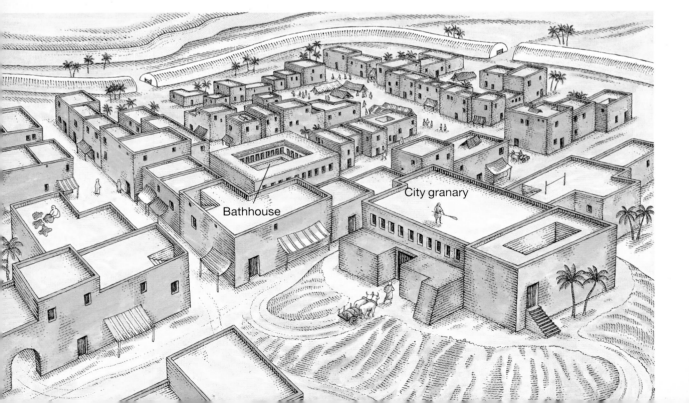

Bathhouse

City granary

Indus Valley grew barley, wheat, melons and dates. Elephants, water buffalo and rhinoceroses roamed the region. The area had many skilled potters, who used the wheel for throwing pots. People also used stone tools, and made knives, weapons, bowls and figures in bronze.

The Indus Valley civilization came to an end about 3500 years ago. No one knows exactly why this civilization ended but possible causes include flooding, as the River Indus changed its course, and attacks from Aryan invaders from the north-west which eventually drove the Indus Valley people away.

▼ Brick-lined shafts like this have been found in the courtyards of houses in Mohenjo-daro. They may have been wells or used to store jars of grain or oil.

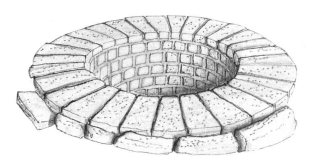

SEALS AND WRITING

More than 1200 seals like this have been found in Mohenjo-daro. They were used by merchants to stamp bales of goods. No one has yet worked out what the writing on them means.

TRADE AND TRADERS

The people of the Indus Valley carried on a busy trade across the Arabian Sea and up the Persian Gulf to Dilmun (now Bahrain). Polished stone weights found at Bahrain are identical to those that have been identified in Mohenjo-daro and Harappa. Soapstone stamping seals used in the Indus Valley have also been found in Bahrain and the ruins of Ur (now in Iraq).

BC

2800–2400 Mesopotamia: The city-states of Sumer are at their most important, with Sumer the known world's richest market.

2750 Sumer: Gilgamesh, legendary king of Uruk, rules.

2750–2000 Construction of the megalithic (huge stone) temples on Malta and Gozo, and excavation of the Hypogeum, an underground rock temple.

2700 England: Construction of the first stage of Stonehenge begins on Salisbury Plain, Wiltshire.

2697 China: Huang Ti, the 'Yellow Emperor' becomes emperor. Indus Valley: Metal working reaches the valley; start of major civilization there.

2630 Djoser becomes pharaoh; his advisor Imhotep designs the Step Pyramid at Saqqara, the first pyramid; it is a series of platforms built one above the other.

Weaving was an important activity for both women and men. This Egyptian loom dates from 1900 BC and was used to weave linen.

2575 Egypt: Beginning of the Old Kingdom from the 4th to the 8th dynasties (to 2134).

2551 Egypt: Khufu (Greek name Cheops) becomes pharaoh and builds the Great Pyramid at Giza. Two other pyramids are built by his successors, Khafre (Chephren) and Menkaure (Mycerinus). The Sphinx at Giza is also built.

BC

c. 2500 Egypt: The first mummies are embalmed. Europe: Metal working spreads through the continent. Norway: The first picture of skiing is made – a rock carving in southern Norway. Scotland: Village of Skara Brae, in Orkney, is destroyed by a sandstorm.

2360 Sumer: Sargon the Great of Akkad begins the conquest of Sumer, and founds the Akkadian empire, the largest to date (lasts until 2180).

This Bronze Age rock engraving from Scandinavia shows a sledge with some animals, probably oxen or deer. It was made by chipping away the surface rock.

2300 The chief priestess of Sumer, Enheduanna, daughter of Sargon I, composes a hymn in praise of Inanna, the Great Mother-Goddess.

2300 Mesopotamia: Semites from Arabia migrate to Mesopotamia and begin to set up the Babylonian and Assyrian kingdoms.

2205 China: According to tradition, this is the period of the Hsia dynasty; Yu is the emperor.

This three-legged earthenware pot was made in China in the 2nd century BC on a potter's wheel.

The Great Migrations

All through history people have been on the move. As populations expand some people travel to places where there is more room for them. They also tend to move as the climate becomes colder or dryer.

By 500,000 years ago humans had spread to all parts of Africa, southern Europe and southern Asia. During the last Ice Age when the sea level was lower, even isolated parts of the world, such as Australia, were occupied.

But the biggest movement, and growth of the number of people, came when the last Ice Age ended and the sea level rose. People began moving north, both in North America and Europe to occupy the now ice-free land.

A great change took place to the east of the Atlantic Ocean around 4000 years ago. A group of peoples known as Indo-Europeans or Aryans moved from their homeland in southern Russia. Some Indo-Europeans travelled south into

VEHICLES

The Indo-Europeans from southern Russia lived on the Steppes (the wide plains). They were wanderers who travelled with their families and possessions in wagons covered with felt. These wagons also served as living quarters. The wagon wheels were made of solid oak boards pegged together, though later spokes were used.

The wagons were drawn by pairs of oxen. From such wagons the war chariot evolved.

▲ *Nomads made camp from time to time so that their animals could graze the rich grass. When it was all eaten, the nomads travelled on. They moved to low ground in winter and higher ground in summer.*

▼ *This map shows the main movements of people in Europe and the Near East after the end of the Ice Age. The arrows indicate the direction in which the Indo-European and Semitic peoples moved.*

what is now Iran (the name is adapted from the word 'Aryan'), and from there into India. Others moved into Anatolia and the Fertile Crescent. A further group of Indo-Europeans occupied the Balkan peninsula and Greece and the Celts later spread into western Europe.

The Indo-Europeans came into conflict with Semitic people (a group of people who all speak a Semitic language, such as Arabic, Hebrew, Akkadian and Phoenician) who had migrated into the Fertile Crescent earlier and settled in Sumer. These Semitic people also moved about, particularly the Hebrews.

In the East, China too was affected by migrations. After 2000 BC, people from central Asia invaded the area several times. However, China remained fairly isolated from the rest of the world.

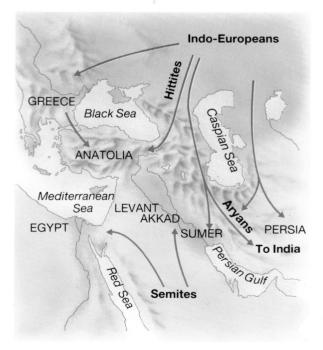

People

The first people worked a few hours a day, hunting, trapping and gathering food. They wore animal skins to keep warm and spent their free time making works of art and jewellery to decorate their bodies. Once people settled down in farming communities, all their time was taken up with agriculture to feed a growing population.

However, as cities grew up and flourished, rich men and women dressed to be fashionable. They looked at themselves in mirrors made of glassy rock called obsidian. Egyptians used cosmetics and wore perfumed wax cones on their heads; as the wax melted it released the perfume. Rich people entertained themselves by playing board games similar to chess and draughts, and listened to music. The Chinese had a musical instrument rather like a huge xylophone, made from jade or bronze.

In contrast, poor people were too busy working to care about fashion and entertainment. For both rich and poor, however, life was short. Many children died as babies and adults often died from accidents or diseases before they were thirty.

► *Egyptian children had many games and toys. Games, with balls made of leather, or wood, were very popular. There were also toys with moving parts, like this wooden lion and wheeled horse.*

▲ *Egyptian noblewomen wore a pleated robe over a straight shift of fine linen. Rich women used cosmetics and perfume. All social classes wore sandals.*

▲ *Minoan noblewomen wore long, flounced skirts with a tight-fitting bodice which had short sleeves. A shaped metal belt pinched in the waist. The cloth was very colourful.*

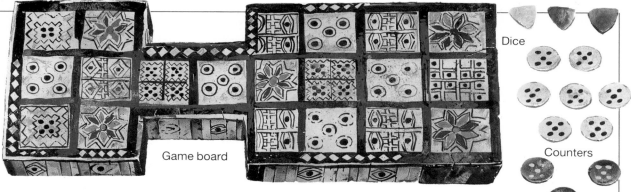

Game board

Dice

Counters

▲ A gaming board, counters and dice dating from between 3000 and 2000 BC. Sadly the rules of the game have not survived.

▲ An Egyptian cosmetic spoon and comb. The comb was worn in the hair for decoration.

▼ The Chinese particularly valued jade and carved a lot of jewellery from it, like this open ring.

▲ Sumerian princesses wore elaborate head-dresses, ear-rings and necklaces, made of gold and silver, decorated with lapis-lazuli and carnelians.

▲ Etruscan women wore a long straight garment with sleeves. It was sometimes gathered at the waist with a sash. They liked to trim their clothes with coloured braid.

Ancient Crete

The very first European civilization began on the island of Crete about 4500 years ago. It is called the Minoan civilization after the legendary king Minos. Stories say that he built a labyrinth (maze) in which he kept a monster known as the Minotaur. It had the head of a bull and the body of a man. The Minoan civilization was at its height from 2200 to 1450 BC. The Minoans owed their prosperity to their abilities as seafarers and traders.

The Minoans built several large cities, connected by paved roads. At the heart of each city was a palace, with a water supply, good drainage, windows and stone seats. The capital, Knossos, had the grandest palace. It had splendid apartments for the king and queen, rooms for religious ceremonies, workshops and a school. The internal walls were plastered and decorated with magnificent painted pictures. Minoan craftsmen were renowned for their skills as potters and builders. They also made

ATLANTIS

The Aegean island of Thera (Santorini) suddenly blew up about 3500 years ago. It was one of the most violent volcanic eruptions in history and it caused a huge tidal wave. This wave swept across the Aegean Sea and the Mediterranean Sea, causing great damage wherever it struck land.

The disappearance of most of Thera gave rise to the legend of the lost land of Atlantis. The Greek philosopher Plato said Atlantis had sunk into the sea because its people were so wicked.

▼ Decorating one of the state rooms at the royal palace at Knossos. The wall painting shows the dangerous sport of bull leaping, which may have given rise to the legend of the Minotaur.

▲ This map shows where the Minoan civilization was located. The Minoans greatly influenced other Aegean civilizations, especially the Mycenaeans who developed later on the Greek mainland.

▼ *A view of the royal palace at Knossos as it looked in Minoan times. It was built of stone and wood and the royal apartments lay around a central courtyard, with public rooms upstairs.*

beautiful jewellery from silver and gold.

The advanced Minoan civilization came to a sudden and mysterious end in about 1450 BC. Its collapse followed the eruption of a huge volcano on the island of Thera (Santorini) which overwhelmed much of Crete. Knossos was invaded by the Mycenaeans who greatly admired the Minoans and took back their ideas to the European mainland.

SHIPBUILDING

Minoan craftsmen were skilled at shipbuilding. In ships like the one shown below, Cretan traders travelled to other islands in the Aegean Sea and to eastern Mediterranean countries, including Egypt. Minoan artefacts, such as their beautiful pottery and metal work have been found in many lands. These finds show that trade for the Cretans was very profitable. It contributed to their great wealth.

BC

2200 Crete: Greek speakers arrive on the island; they use a Minoan script known as Linear A (which is still undeciphered) and Linear B, an early form of Greek writing (deciphered in 1952). Japan: The Jomon culture flourishes.

2150 Indus Valley: First invasion by Aryans from the north.

***c.* 2100** Mesopotamia: The Hebrew patriarch Abraham migrates north and west from Ur. Indus Valley: Aryans continue their invasion.

2040 Egypt: Start of the Middle Kingdom. Lasts to the end of the 14th dynasty (1640).

2030 Mesopotamia: The decline of Sumer is now under way.

The double-axe, labrys, was a symbol of Crete's mother-goddess and was painted on the walls throughout the palace at Knossos.

2000 Indo-Europeans (early Greeks) invade and settle mainland Greece. Minoan Crete dominates the Aegean Sea region; Minoans start building the palace at Knossos. Anatolia: Hittites, an Indo-European tribe, move in; they monopolize the secret of working iron. Egypt: Locks and latches come into use. Europe: The Bronze Age begins. England: Construction of the second stage of Stonehenge begins. Scotland: Work begins on erecting the Ring of Brodgar, a stone circle in Orkney. Peru: Cotton is cultivated. New Guinea: First settlers arrive.

1950 Assyria: Building begins of a great temple and palace at Mari. Egypt: Armies of Pharaoh Sesostris I invade Canaan (land west of the River Jordan). Mesopotamia: Decline of the empire of Ur.

1920 Anatolia: Assyrian merchants establish a colony at Cappadocia (to 1850).

BC

1900–1600 Greece: Development of the Mycenaean culture.

1800 Micronesia: First settlers arrive.

1830 Babylon: Founding of the first dynasty. Its armies conquer the city-states of northern and southern Mesopotamia.

1792 Babylon: Accession of Hammurabi the Great, who produces a code of laws (reign lasts to 1750).

1783–1550 Anatolia (Turkey): Old Kingdom of the Hittites.

1760 China: Shang dynasty is founded.

1700 Syria: Invasion by the Hittites. England: Third phase of building Stonehenge begins.

1650–1450 Greece: Growth of Mycenaean power, centred on Mycenae and Pylos.

Mycenaean nobles were buried in 'beehive' tombs. This one is called the Treasury of Atreus and was found at Mycenae in Greece.

1640 Egypt: The Hyksos, a Semitic tribe, begin the conquest of the country, founding the 15th dynasty; about this time the Israelites settle in Egypt, possibly under Hyksos protection.

1600 Mycenaeans trade by sea throughout the Mediterranean. Syria: The Hittites capture Aleppo on Mediterranean coast.

1550 Egypt: Beginning of the New Kingdom (till 1070); the Hyksos are driven out; Temple of Amun at Karnak is begun.

1504–1450 Egypt: Period of expansion under Tuthmosis I, who soon controls Palestine, Syria, and south along the Nile into Kush (Nubia). Mexico: Stone temples built.

The Mycenaeans

Mycenae was a city in Peloponnesus, the southern peninsula of Greece. It was the centre of the first Greek civilization, which grew up at about the same time as that of the Minoans in Crete. The city has given its name to the whole of the late Bronze Age in Greece.

The Mycenaean civilization originally began as a series of little hillside villages, occupied by people speaking an ancient form of Greek. In time many villages grew into great fortified towns, with palaces and luxurious goods that rivalled those made by the highly-skilled craftsmen of King Minos.

Before they built fortresses the Mycenaeans began to bury their important people in elaborate graves, known as 'beehive tombs' from their shape. These tombs were built of large

---

AGAMEMNON AND THE TROJAN WAR

Homer's epic poem the *Iliad* tells the story of the Greek siege of Troy, a city lying on the coast of Anatolia. Paris, son of the king of Troy, eloped with Helen, the wife of Menelaus who was king of Sparta. Menelaus's brother Agamemnon, King of Mycenae, raised an army to attack Troy and get Helen back. Much of the story is legend, but Troy existed, and Agamemnon was almost certainly a real king of Mycenae. This gold mask was found in a grave at Mycenae by a German archaeologist, Heinrich Schliemann. He thought it was the mask of Agamemnon, but today scholars think it was that of a man who lived 300 years earlier.

stone blocks, shaped to form a great dome. One tomb at Mycenae, known as the Treasury of Atreus, has a doorway nearly 6 metres high, opening into a chamber more than 13 metres high and 14 metres wide. It was once lined with bronze plates.

The richness of these tombs shows that a great deal of money and effort was spent on royalty and the aristocracy. To judge by the treasures found in many of the tombs, wealthy Mycenaeans were very fond of gold, imported from Egypt. Craftsmen made golden cups, masks, flowers, jewellery, and inlaid swords and armour with gold. It is no wonder that the poet Homer described Mycenae as 'rich in gold'.

LION GATE

The ruins of the Lion Gate which was the main entrance into Mycenae and was built around 1300 BC. It was almost the only way through the city walls, which were built of great stone boulders. The lions, now without their heads, stand above a massive stone lintel (beam). Walls flanked the way to the Lion Gate, so that defenders could attack an enemy on both sides. The walls were built at a time when Mycenae was threatened with attacks from the north, but they did not save Mycenae from destruction.

◄ The map shows the world as the Mycenaeans knew it, with the Aegean Sea bounded by Greece to the west and Anatolia to the east.

▼ A reconstruction of the city of Mycenae as it probably looked at the height of its power. The royal palace on the hilltop was built on several levels.

BC

1500 Crete: Minoans are facing growing competition from Mycenae. Indus Valley civilization: Aryan invaders destroy Mohenjo-daro. Anatolia: The Hittite royal succession becomes hereditary; Hittites control all Anatolia.

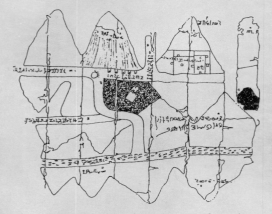

This piece of a sketch map comes from the only surviving ancient Egyptian map and is thought to show the quarries and goldmines of the Wadi Hammamat in the Eastern Desert.

1500 China: The first historical period begins under the Shang dynasty; Anyang becomes the capital. Bronze is worked in the Anyang region.

1500–1000 India: Early civilization spreads along the Ganges river valley.

1479 Egypt: Pharaoh Tuthmosis II is succeeded by the young child Tuthmosis III but his aunt, Hatshepsut, effectively rules for the first 22 years of his reign.

c. 1473 Battle of Megiddo – Tuthmosis III of Egypt conquers Palestine.

1470 Explosion of the volcano Thera in the Aegean Sea causes widespread damage, particularly in Crete.

1450 Collapse of Minoan power begins, probably as a consequence of volcanic or earthquake damage.

1430–1200 New Kingdom of the Hittites.

1400 Crete: Knossos, the Minoan capital, is destroyed by fire. Mycenaeans occupy the island. Egypt: Temples at Luxor are under construction. India and western Asia: Iron Age under way.

Shang Dynasty

Early civilizations in China grew up on the banks of the three largest rivers: the Huang He (Yellow River), the Chang Jiang (Yangtze) and the Xi Jiang (West River). Like the people of Mesopotamia and Egypt, Chinese farmers relied on the rivers for water to grow their crops and for transport. But they faced two dangers: devastating floods and raids by people from the north. The invaders were the Xiung-Nu (Huns or Mongols).

The first years of China's history are a mixture of fact and legend. According to tradition the first dynasty (ruling family) was the Hsia, who came to power more than 4000 years ago. The first Hsia emperor was named Yu and he is credited with taming the rivers by building dykes (banks) to keep the floods at bay and building channels to supply

---

SILK

Tradition says that silk was discovered in about 2690 BC by the Empress Hsi-Ling Shi, the wife of the legendary 'Yellow Emperor', Huang Ti. The empress found that the silkworms ate the leaves of mulberry trees so she had groves of mulberries planted to feed the insects.

Because the empress cultivated silkworms, the ladies of her court did so too. Silk was so valuable that for centuries it was used as a form of money. It remained a closely kept secret by the Chinese for about 3000 years.

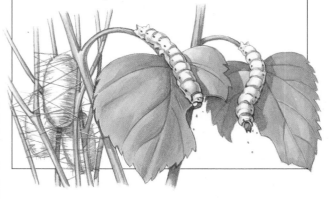

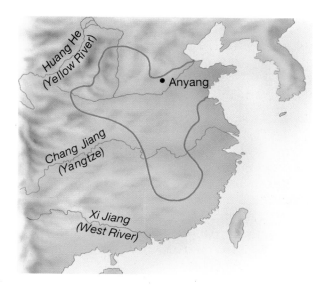

▲ *The map shows the area ruled by the Shang. According to tradition the Hsia ruled before the Shang but no historical evidence has yet been found to support this belief.*

▶ *The early Chinese were a warlike people. Shang warriors fought in cumbersome body armour, largely made of bamboo and wood, heavily padded with cloth.*

BRONZE

Shang metal-workers made this bronze cauldron. It was used in religious ceremonies of ancestor worship. Many of the bronze vessels made by the Shang were cast in moulds. The craft workers decorated them with wavy lines and sometimes with symbolic human faces.

ORACLE BONE

Large numbers of animal bones like this have been excavated near the city of Anyang. They are engraved with the earliest examples of Chinese writing. Many of these bones were used for telling fortunes and are called oracle bones. The bones used were mostly shoulder blades.

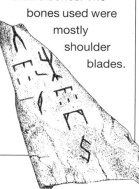

the land with regular supplies of water.

The first dynasty we know about for certain was called the Shang, and their first emperor was named T'ang. The Shang dynasty ruled in China for more than 400 years. The people grew millet, wheat, some rice and also mulberries. They kept cattle, pigs, sheep, dogs and chickens, and hunted deer and wild boar. The Shang also used horses to draw ploughs and chariots.

Religion

From earliest times, people tried to come to terms with things they could not explain, such as birth, disease and death. The first religions probably came out of this. Over 50,000 years ago, Neanderthal people buried some of their dead with flowers. The first farmers wanted good harvests every year. They probably asked for help from nature gods, such as the Sun and the Moon. However, nothing is known for certain until the time of the Sumerians. Some of the temples they built to their nature gods eventually became the centres of cities.

▲ A boundary stone from Babylon, carved with prayers asking the gods to protect the owner's land.

► Ishtar was the goddess of war to the Assyrians, but a mother-goddess to the Babylonians.

▲ People first worshipped mother-goddesses who, as the Earth, gave life to all living things.

▲ *Sumerian legends contain many well known stories. The Great Flood was sent to punish men who had made the gods* angry. *They warned one good man, Ut-napishtim, to build a boat. The flood destroyed everything on Earth except the boat. Ut-* napishtim sent out birds to find land. Finally one bird did not return and Ut-napishtim and his family were saved.

CREATION MYTHS

Every civilization had its own story to explain the creation of the Earth. These stories are called myths. The Egyptians thought the world started as a watery chaos. The Sun god Atum emerged from it and created the gods of air and moisture. They had a daughter, Nut, who was the sky goddess. Her brother Geb was the Earth god and also her husband.

◄ *The ancient Chinese cooked sacrificial food for their dead ancestors in large bronze vessels like this one.*

▼ *The Egyptians believed in life after death. The mummified bodies of their pharaohs were buried with boats symbolizing the journey to the next world. Royal tombs were also filled with food, jewellery, clothing and statues of servants.*

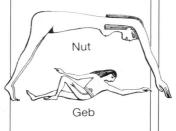

Nut

Geb

BC

1391–1353 Egypt: The reign of Amenhotep III, the country's 'Golden Age'; he makes his capital at Thebes into a magnificent city and begins the Temple of Luxor and erects the Colossi of Memnon.

1390–1350 Anatolia: The Hittites, led by Suppiluliumas, their greatest king, reconquer Anatolia, subdue northern Syria and make the Mitanni tribes into Hittite subjects.

1366 Assyria: Assuruballit I becomes king and begins Assyria's rise to power in Mesopotamia.

1353 Egypt: Accession of Amenhotep III's son Amenhotep IV, who begins the worship of the god Aten; he takes the name Akhenaten and abolishes the other gods.

1333 Egypt: The boy-king Tutankhamun succeeds Akhenaten; his advisers restore the worship of the traditional Egyptian gods; Tutankhamun lives only a few years (to 1323), but his tomb survives almost intact until AD 1922.

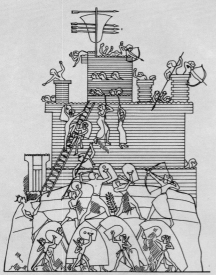

A wall-carving showing Egyptian troops attacking the Hittite fortress of Dapur.

1308 Assyria: Accession of Adadnirari I, who embarks on a career of conquest.

1307 Egypt: Pharaoh Ramesses I founds the vigorous 19th dynasty.

The Hittites

The Hittites appear suddenly in the pages of history. They arrived in Anatolia, probably from further east, but we do not know whether they made one invasion or migrated gradually. They were made up of several tribes and spoke as many as six languages.

For many years the Hittites controlled the supply of iron, and this, together with their use of chariots, gave this warlike people a great advantage. They conquered northern Syria, Mesopotamia and Babylon before being overwhelmed by the Assyrians in about 1200 BC.

▲ *Rock carvings left by the Hittites tell us that they were a very warlike race. Here a king hunts lions.*

▼ *The map shows the extent of the Hittite empire at its height under Suppiluliumas in about 1350 BC.*

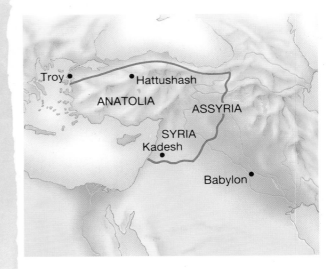

Babylon

The end of the Sumerian domination of Mesopotamia was followed by a series of invasions. About 3800 years ago the Babylonians shook off their rulers, and their king Sumuabum founded a dynasty that lasted for 300 years.

They began to dominate southern Mesopotamia under their sixth ruler, Hammurabi the Great. He was a highly efficient ruler. The armies of Babylonia were well-disciplined, and they conquered in turn the city-states of Isin, Elam and Larsa, and the strong kingdom of Mari which lay on the Euphrates.

The mathematicians of Babylonia devised a system of counting based on the number 60, from which we get the number of minutes in an hour and the degrees (60 x 6) in a circle.

▼ Gilgamesh was the legendary hero of a poem called The Epic of Gilgamesh. *Here Gilgamesh sleeps and loses the plant of eternal life to a snake.*

HAMMURABI

Hammurabi is famous for the laws he introduced. They were designed to protect the weak from the strong, and they covered all daily activities including rates of pay and rules of trade. People who broke the law faced severe punishments.

▼ This map shows the extent of the Babylonian empire under Hammurabi and his successors.

The Assyrians

While Babylonia ruled in southern Mesopotamia, the fierce and warlike Assyrians dominated the north. Their kingdom lay in the valley of the River Tigris. Its capital Assur was named after the Assyrians' chief god.

King Adadnirari I, the country's first powerful ruler, enlarged the Assyrian empire and took the boastful title 'King of Everything'. He and his successors were cruel dictators, ruling their empire as a whole and not allowing individual states independence. As the empire grew, rebellions were common.

Assyria's first period of power lasted for nearly 300 years. It reached its height under King Tiglathpileser I, who led brutal campaigns of conquest every year. From about 1100 BC, Assyria and Babylonia were overrun by Aramaic tribes from northern Syria. But a hundred years or so later, Assurdan II and his successors reconquered the Assyrian empire. It reached its greatest size under Tiglathpileser III.

The last great ruler of Assyria was King

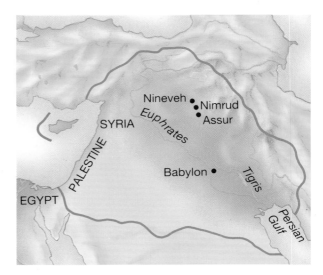

▲ The Assyrian empire at its greatest extent in 650 BC. It extended from Syria in the north to the Persian Gulf, and included Palestine and most of Egypt. After Egypt and Babylon broke away the empire collapsed.

▼ Under the supervision of their king, Assyrian workers toil to bring materials for building a new palace. Oarsmen in skin boats tow a raft along the Tigris.

Assurbanipal. He had a great love of the arts and during his reign he collected a huge library at his palace in Nineveh, which was then the capital of Assyria. When he died the Assyrian empire collapsed, and by 609 BC it had ended.

The Assyrians were great builders, erecting magnificent cities with temples and palaces. Assyrian men wore long coat-like garments, and were bearded. Women wore a sleeved tunic and draped a shawl over their shoulders. It was not unknown for men to sell their wives and children into slavery to pay off debts.

▲ A battle scene carved on limestone shows warriors on a camel fighting off an attack by Assyrian foot soldiers carrying spears, bows and arrows.

LANGUAGE

The Assyrians spoke Aramaic, a language related to Hebrew and Arabic. It was the language spoken by Jesus. For a long time Assyrians wrote on clay tablets, using the cuneiform script which the Babylonians developed from earlier Sumerian. When parchment came into use they wrote on that in ink. Thousands of tablets have survived, but few parchments.

ASSURBANIPAL

Assurbanipal ruled Assyria from 668 to 627 BC. He was a ruthless soldier but also a great patron of the arts. He built a splendid palace at Nineveh and filled the gardens with plants from all over the world.

BC

1305 Egypt: Ramesses I's son Seti I sets out to reconquer lands in Palestine and Syria.

1300 Iran: Medes and Persians invade. Egypt: Construction of the great rock temples of Abu Simbel begins; oppression of the Israelite colony in Egypt. Phoenicia: Sidon flourishes as a great port. Greece: The Arcadians begin settling central Peloponnesus. England: The last phase of Stonehenge is completed. Melanesia: First settlers arrive.

1290 Egypt: Accession of Ramesses II, the Great; Commandment carved on the base of a giant statue of the pharaoh refers to 'the Royal Mother, the Mistress of the World'.

The Assyrian winged lion from Assurbanipal's palace was thought to ward off evil.

1298 Assyria: Adadnirari I reaches the Euphrates and takes the title 'King of Everything'.

1285 Battle of Kadesh between Egypt and the Hittites: both sides claim victory.

1283 Peace between Egypt and the Hittites.

1275 Assyria: Shalmaneser I becomes ruler, and extends Assyria's conquests.

c. 1270 The Exodus: the Israelites under Moses leave Egypt; they move into Canaan (Palestine) and adopt the worship of the one god, Yahweh.

c. 1250 Anatolia: City of Troy besieged by Greek army.

1232–1116 Assyria: Period of decline followed by new growth of power.

1232 Israelites in Canaan (Palestine): an Egyptian army under Ramesses II's son Merneptah defeats them in battle.

BC

1200–800 India: Aryan invaders worship nature gods; they raise cattle and cultivate crops.

1200 Israel (Canaan): Period of the Judges begins; the prophetess Deborah flourishes. Anatolia: Invasion by the Sea People, a confederation of Philistines, Greeks, Sardinians and Sicilians; the Hittite empire collapses. Sahara: Horses and chariots are in use on trade routes.

The Phoenicians sent wood from Cedar of Lebanon trees to build Solomon's temple.

1194 Egypt: Ramesses III becomes pharaoh and founds the 20th dynasty with its capital at Tanis.

1179 Egypt is invaded by the Confederation of Sea Peoples, which is defeated by Ramesses III.

1170 The Levant (eastern Mediterranean coast): growing power of newly independent Phoenician cities, especially Tyre.

1150–1100 Greece: Collapse of Mycenaean power.

1140 The Phoenicians create their first North African colony at Utica, which is now in Tunisia.

1125 Babylonia: the armies of Nebuchadnezzar I hold off renewed attacks by the Assyrians.

The Origin of the Jews

The Hebrews who settled in Palestine about 4000 years ago were a tribe that came from southern Mesopotamia. Their name literally meant 'the people from the other side' of the Euphrates river. Their story is told in the Bible.

According to the Old Testament, the first Hebrew was Abraham, a shepherd who lived in Ur. Abraham travelled with his family, first to Syria and then to Canaan (the old name for Palestine), where he settled. His grandson, Jacob, had 12 sons after whom the 12 Hebrew tribes were named. When famine struck Canaan, Jacob led his people to safety in Egypt. Jacob was also called Israel, and the Hebrews became known as Israelites. Later they became slaves of the Egyptians until Moses, a religious leader, took them back to Canaan. There they fought the Philistines to establish the land of Israel.

After around 1020 BC the Israelites prospered under three kings, Saul, David

▼ *The two Hebrew kingdoms of Israel and Judah.*

SOLOMON

Solomon was one of the wisest kings in history. Despite leading a life of luxury, he always carried out his royal duties. His rule brought order and peace and Jerusalem was one of the richest cities of the time.

and Solomon. David united the tribes of Israel into one nation and made the city of Jerusalem his capital. After Solomon died, the kingdom split into two: Israel and Judah. The Assyrians captured Israel in 722 BC and Judah in 683 BC. From then on, the people were called Jews.

▲ *This copy of an Egyptian wall-painting shows a group of Hebrews asking permission to enter Egypt.*

▼ *Solomon built the first temple in Jerusalem to house the Israelites' holy treasure, the Ark of the Covenant which contained the Ten Commandments. It became the focus of the cult following the one god, Yahweh.*

Science and Technology

The early history of the world is often divided into periods which are named after the technology which was in use at the time. The three main divisions are Stone Age, Bronze Age and Iron Age. These divisions cover different periods of time in different parts of the world. For example, in ancient China the Bronze Age started around 2700 BC and lasted for over 2000 years, while in Africa the Iron Age started around 800 BC and followed straight on from the Stone Age. Apart from metal making, probably the most important early invention was the wheel.

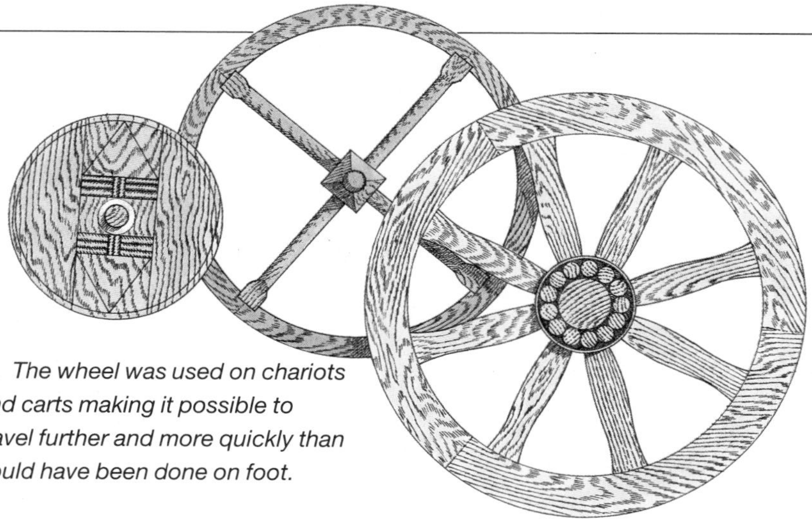

▲ *The wheel was used on chariots and carts making it possible to travel further and more quickly than could have been done on foot.*

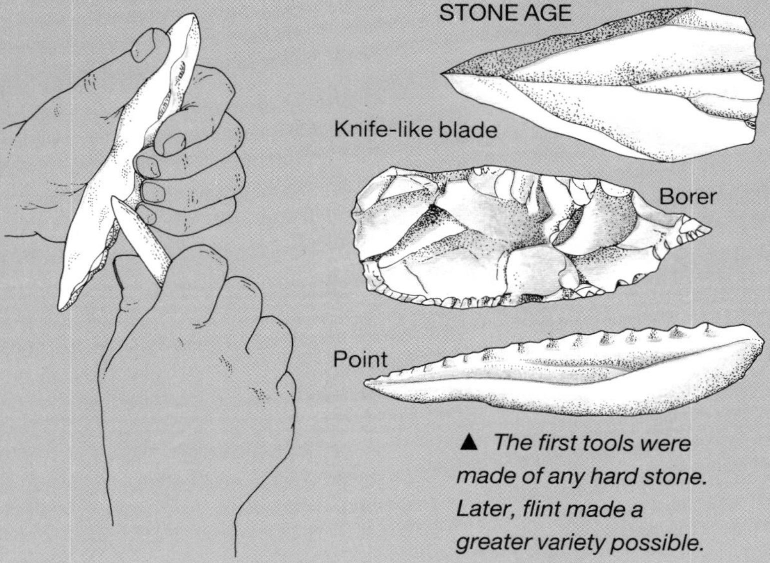

STONE AGE

Knife-like blade

Borer

Point

▲ *The first tools were made of any hard stone. Later, flint made a greater variety possible.*

▼ *Using wheels in pulleys made it easier to lift heavy loads.*

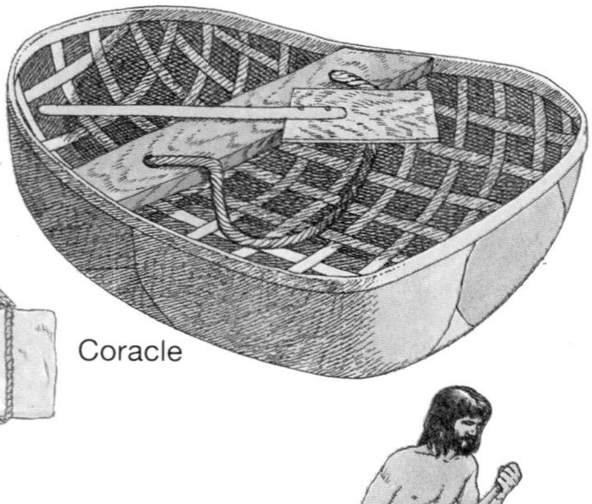

Coracle

◄ *Around 6000 BC coracles made of animal skins fixed to a wooden frame were used as boats in Wales. Below Dug-out canoes made from hollowed logs were used around 8000 BC.*

Dugout canoe

52

◀ The first farmers used ploughs made from wood. The ploughshare was often made from a deer antler or animal bone. It made a furrow in the soil but did not turn it over like modern ploughs do. The earliest ploughs were pulled by people, but later ones were pulled by oxen, as in this scene from Egypt.

BRONZE AGE

Bucket

Axehead

▲ A 7th century BC bronze bucket and bronze axehead, both found on European sites.

Dagger

Sheath

IRON AGE

Nails

Scythe

▲ A Roman scythe for cutting corn and a dagger with its sheath, from Europe.

WHEN IT HAPPENED

c. **9000 BC** Arrowheads first made in Americas.
c. **8000 BC** First farming in Mesopotamia.
c. **3000 BC** The wheel is used on chariots in Mesopotamia.
c. **2700 BC** Chinese start making bronze and weaving silk.
c. **2500 BC** Bricks start to be used for building in the Indus Valley.
c. **1500 BC** Iron is smelted (heating ore to extract metal) by the Hittites, in the Near East.

▶ Early potters' wheels were made from wood. The turntable was fixed to a spindle which was turned by a foot wheel.

Egypt, the New Kingdom

A succession of feeble rulers in Egypt left the country open to an attack. It came from the Hyksos, a tribe of herdsmen from Canaan. They invaded Egypt and became its 'shepherd kings', founding the 13th to the 17th dynasties. They ruled for more than a hundred years, until a group of rebellious Egyptian princes drove them out and set up the 18th dynasty.

The 18th dynasty marked the beginning of Egypt's 'golden age', which is known as the New Kingdom. One of its early pharaohs, Tuthmosis III, conquered Palestine, Syria and all the lands west of the Euphrates. During the rule of Amenhotep III, the New Kingdom, which had its capital at Thebes, became rich and prosperous.

The strangest ruler was Amenhotep IV. He made Aten, the Sun in the sky, the chief god of Egypt. He changed his name to Akhenaten and even moved his capital to a new city devoted to Aten and its worship. His queen was Nefertiti, who was not of royal birth and may not have

HATSHEPSUT

Queen Hatshepsut was an early ruler of the New Kingdom. Widow of a weak king, Tuthmosis II, she ruled as queen in her own right, and was depicted with the false beard of a pharaoh.

▼ *Models found in the tomb of Tutankhamun provide a vivid picture of the life of Egyptian people during the age of the New Kingdom.*

◄ *This temple at Abu Simbel was carved out of rock on the banks of the Nile. Four figures of Ramesses II guard the entrance. It was moved in 1964 to avoid flooding when the Aswan High Dam was built.*

been Egyptian. When Akhenaten died the people returned to their old gods.

Ordinary farmers and workers lived simply but the nobility had a far more luxurious lifestyle. In law men and women were equal and women could own property and do as they wished with it. Women could choose to follow one of four professions: as priestesses, midwives, dancers and mourners. The children of the aristocracy were well educated, especially the boys. Apart from the nobles, scribes and priests held the most important positions in Egyptian society of the time.

◄ *The dead bodies of pharaohs and nobles were embalmed so that they would 'live' forever, a process called mummification. The body was put inside a coffin like this one with a portrait painted on the outside.*

TUTANKHAMUN'S TOMB

Pharaohs were buried with many possessions in elaborate tombs such as the pyramids. But from very early on these were plundered by robbers. Thinking that it would be safer, pharaohs were then buried in the cliffs of the Valley of the Kings. Even so only one of these has survived to the present day, that of the boy-king Tutankhamun. He succeeded Akhenaten but died when he was only 18. He was buried surrounded by treasure and beautiful furniture. This gold mask covered his face.

BC

1122 China: Emperor Wu Wang founds the Zhou dynasty and establishes a feudal system.

1116 Assyria: Tiglathpileser I rules; he fights off invaders from the north, conquers Babylon and controls Asian trade.

Queen Hatshepsut had this mortuary temple built for herself at Deir el Bahri.

1100–1050 Greece is invaded by Dorian and Ionian tribes from the north, bringing with them the use of iron swords and destroying the Mycenaean citadels.

1100–900 Babylonia: Aramaic tribes invade. China: The first Chinese-language dictionary is compiled.

1093–935 Assyria and Babylonia are both overrun by Aramaeans.

1087 Egypt: The high priests of Amun become the effective rulers under a succession of weak pharaohs.

1070 Egypt: The New Kingdom ends with the death of Ramesses XI; Smendes, a rich merchant, becomes pharaoh and founds the 21st dynasty; for a time Egypt splits into two kingdoms. Israel is conquered by the Philistines, who settle in Palestine. Greece: The Dorians and Ionians invade Peloponnesus.

Akhenaten with his wife Nefertiti and some of their children. Akhenaten worshipped Aten, 'the sun-disk'.

1045 Greece: Death of Codron, the legendary last king of Athens, possibly killed in battle with the Dorians.

The Phoenicians

The Phoenicians were merchants, pirates, and the greatest seafarers of the ancient world. They lived along the coastal strip at the eastern end of the Mediterranean Sea, often known as the Levant, and now part of Syria, Lebanon and Israel. Their language was related to Babylonian and Hebrew.

They were originally called Canaanites, because they lived in the land of Canaan. From about 1200 BC they were called Phoenicians from the Greek word *phoinos*, or red, because they produced a wonderful reddish-purple dye.

The Phoenicians' main port was Tyre, which according to tradition they founded 4750 years ago. The city had close links with Israel. Hiram, king of Tyre, supplied Solomon with cedar wood and craftsmen to build the Temple in Jerusalem and Ahab, king of Israel married Jezebel, Princess of Tyre.

▲ This is how a Phoenician warship probably looked. It was a galley with a ram for attacking other ships. It could use wind power with its square sail, and its oars made it highly manoeuvrable.

▼ The bold sailors of Phoenicia founded many colonies along the coasts of the Mediterranean. They traded throughout that sea, and even ventured into the Atlantic to Britain and down the African coast.

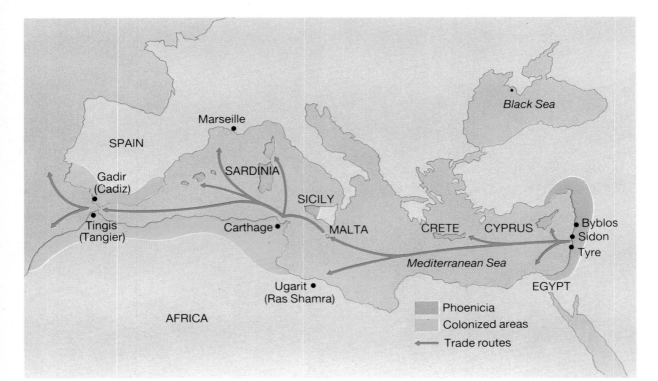

56

ALPHABET

The Phoenicians were among the first people to use an alphabet. Theirs had 30 letters, all consonants. Their alphabet is the basis of the one we use today. The word Bible comes from the name Byblos, the name of a Phoenician port. The Greeks took it as their word for book.

CARTHAGE

Carthage was founded by Dido, the daughter of a king of Tyre. When she landed in North Africa, she asked the local ruler for land. He said she could have as much land as an ox-hide would cover. Dido had the hide cut into very thin strips so that she was able to mark off a large area of land.

The Phoenicians were skilled craft workers, making glassware, weapons, jewellery and cloth. They traded these goods all along the Mediterranean coasts and imported goods from such far away places as Britain.

Their trading helped to spread scientific knowledge and technology. They set up many colonies, the most important being Carthage (now in Tunisia). Other colonies were Marseille (France), Cadiz (Spain), and Malta, Sicily and Cyprus.

GLASSWARE AND PURPLE DYE

The Phoenicians were the first people to make, on a large scale, transparent glass, like this perfume bottle. They invented the process of glass-blowing. They made the dye for which Tyre was famous (Tyrian purple, a rich dark violet shade) from a gland in the murex, a sea snail. Cloth dyed in this rich colour was expensive, and it was worn by Greeks and Romans as a sign of rank. But the process of making it was smelly. Other peoples did not like to visit Tyre because of the tremendous garlic-like stench.

BC

1020 Israel: Samuel, last of the Judges, anoints Saul as the first king of the Israelites; Saul leads a successful revolt against the Philistines.

1000–774 Phoenicia: Great period of Tyre.

1000–950 China: The Western Zhou dynasty establishes its capital at Hao in the Wei Valley.

1000 Israel: Saul is killed at the battle of Gilboa; he is succeeded by David, first as king of Judah, later as king of Israel.

India: The *Rig Veda*, a Hindu religious text containing sacred hymns, is compiled about this time; iron tools are made in the Ganges Valley. Phoenicia: The people of Tyre employ a full alphabet. Greeks establish colonies in the Aegean islands.

A murex sea snail, from whose glands a purple dye was made.

1000–600 Italy: The Villanova culture flourishes at this time.

994 Israel: David captures Jerusalem and makes it his capital. Central Europe: Teutonic tribes move westward to the River Rhine.

961 Israel: Death of David who is succeeded by his son Solomon; development of trade, laws and taxes.

The Phoenicians were famous for ivory carvings, like this head of a young girl.

BC

953 Israel: Dedication of the Temple at Jerusalem, built by Solomon with help and materials from Hiram of Tyre.

935 Revival of Assyria begins with the accession of Assurdan II: by 860 he and his successors Adadnirari, Tukultinurta and Assurnasirapli II have re-established Assyria's ancient boundaries.

922 Israel: Death of Solomon, who is succeeded by his son, Rehoboam; a rebellion against Rehoboam's rule is led by his brother Jeroboam; Solomon's kingdom is split into Judah in the south, under Rehoboam, and Israel in the north under Jeroboam.

An African necklace made from beads and animal teeth.

The warring Assyrians were able to knock holes in stone walls with this battering ram with moveable tower.

900–625 Assyria and Babylon are constantly at war at this time.

900–700 Italy: The Etruscans flourish in upper Italy, a race with a unique language and religion.

***c.* 900** Africa: Kingdom of Kush becomes independent of Egypt. Nok culture of Nigeria begins.

884 Assyria: Centralized government is adopted under Assurnasirapli II.

859 Accession of Assurnasirapli II's son Shalmaneser III (reigns to 825); an ambitious ruler, he launches annual campaigns against neighbouring states.

Africa

Although the earliest human remains have been found in Africa, not much is known of the continent's history before 1500 BC outside Egypt.

Today the Sahara forms a great desert barrier between northern and southern Africa, but in about 6000 BC that barrier did not exist. Rock and cave drawings and paintings show that the climate then was much wetter. One painting shows hunters in a canoe trying to spear a hippopotamus. The Sahara began to dry up after 3500 BC, but trade routes across it remained open, providing a link between northern and southern Africa.

Egyptian culture spread to Nubia, further south along the Nile in what is now northern Sudan. The kingdom of Kush developed in Nubia from 2000 BC onward. Kush was valuable to Egypt as a trading centre. Egypt conquered Kush in 1500 BC, but was in turn conquered by

▼ *The map shows the area of Nubia and the kingdom of Kush and where rock paintings have been found in the Sahara Desert.*

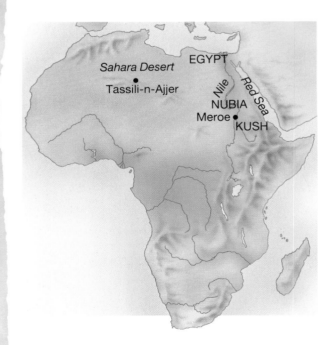

FARMING

On the fringes of the encroaching desert early farmers grew crops such as millet, sorghum and yams. Millet was especially important because it can withstand a drier climate than sorghum. Yams are nutritious tubers. In the Sahara region pastoral peoples herded goats and sheep. Later they kept several kinds of cattle. They roamed from one oasis to another in search of water for their animals.

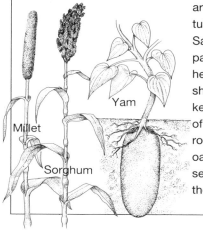

Millet

Sorghum

Yam

the Kushites in *c.* 750 BC, who founded the 25th dynasty of pharaohs.

Kush never had a Bronze Age, but went straight from stone to iron. The capital was moved from Napata to Meroe because Meroe was surrounded by iron ore deposits. It became an important centre of iron working. From Kush the art of iron working spread westward.

▲ *This wall painting from an Egyptian tomb shows a group of Nubians, bearing gifts including fruit, jewellery, furs and monkeys, for the pharaoh. Such paintings show that the Nubians were black Africans.*

▼ *Rock paintings and relief carvings are found all over Africa. This cattle herding scene was painted on a rock in the Tassili-n-Ajjer area in the Sahara. The artist has even recorded the colouring of individual cows.*

Trade

Once people settled down and started farming, they began to make things like pots and baskets. Sometimes they made more than they needed in their own town or village. When this happened, they could exchange these goods for something of equal value from another community. This might be food or raw materials which they did not have in their own village. Sometimes the goods which were traded were very distinctive. By studying them and the places where they were found, archaeologists have worked out ancient trade routes. Goods traded included gold, wine, silk, pottery, grain, woollen cloth and furs. For centuries all these goods were bartered, but slowly tokens came into use. These might be made of clay or shells or beads, or even small ingots of metal such as copper, bronze or iron. Other people paid with cattle or horses. The Chinese probably originally traded with tools such as spades and hoes as their early tokens were shaped like them. The first coins to have a fixed value were used in Anatolia, Turkey, in the Near East around 700 BC.

◄ The first coins were made in Anatolia, Turkey, from electrum, a mixture of gold and silver. The face stamp guaranteed its weight.

◄ Early Chinese money was shaped like a spade.

▼ Sumerian traders had their own cylinder seal for signing contracts.

▼ A storage jar from Knossos in Crete. These jars were used for transporting grain, oil and wine.

▼ As trade grew, people needed to keep records of the goods they bought and sold. The Sumerians wrote theirs on clay tablets like this one.

c. **6000 BC** The people of Çatal Hüyük trade over long distances. Mediterranean shells are traded to make necklaces.

c. **3300 BC** The Sumerians start to use clay tokens in exchange for goods.

c. **1000 BC** By this date the Phoenicians are trading all around the Mediterranean.

c. **700 BC** Coins first used in Lydia, Anatolia in the Near East.

▶ *The Sumerians used clay tokens for trading as shown in this scene. It is thought that there was a different token for each commodity being traded. Of the tokens shown here **1** represents one sheep, **2** one metal ingot, **3** and **4** are unknown, **5** represents one ewe and **6** a jar of oil.*

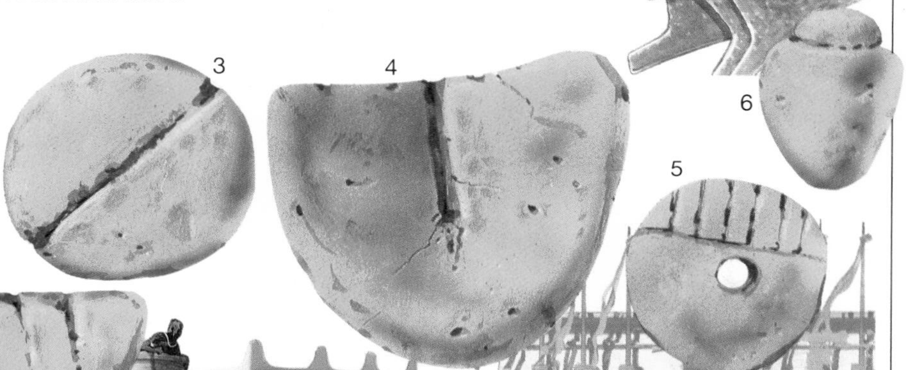

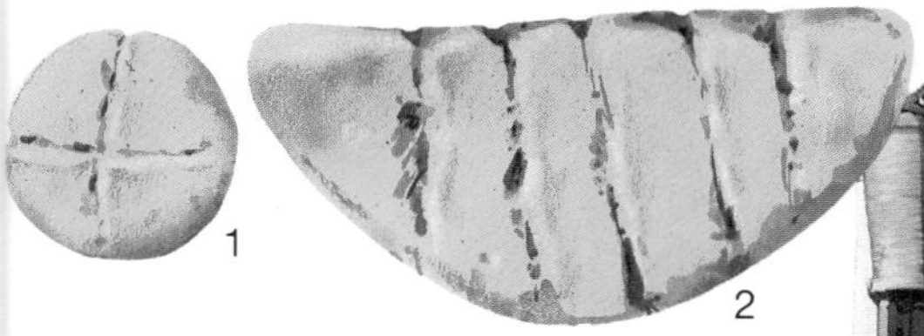

▼ *A Phoenician ship in Egypt. The Phoenicians were long-distance traders and travelled as far as Britain to buy cloth.*

American Civilizations

The first Americans came overland from Asia when the sea level was lower and there was dry land in the Bering Strait. Over thousands of years they spread right to the tip of South America. Many of them remained hunters, fishers and food gatherers, but in two areas civilizations grew up: Mesoamerica (Mexico and Central America) and Peru.

In Mesoamerica some 9000 years ago the Native Americans began to settle down and grow crops such as corn (maize), beans and pumpkins. A series of small villages sprang up, where the people made pottery and wove cloth. From this culture came one of the first civilizations: that of the Olmecs with its centre at La Venta, in western Mexico.

The Olmecs built large earth pyramids as centres for religious worship, and produced huge sculptures and fine jade carvings. Many of their sculptures mix human and jaguar-like features. The

BC

854 Assyria: Shalmaneser III attacks the lands of Palestine: Ahab of Israel, Ben Hadad I of Damascus, and Irkhuleni of Hamath lead an allied army to halt his advance, supported by Egypt and Jehoshaphat of Judah.

850 Peru: The Chavín culture flourishes (to 500).

842 Israel: Jehu, a soldier, leads a rebellion against Ahab's son Jehoram, and founds a new dynasty.

814 North Africa: The Phoenicians establish the city of Carthage (literally 'new town') near their colony of Utica; other Phoenician colonies are set up in Sicily and Spain.

810 Assyria: Sammuramat (the Semiramis of legend) rules as regent for her son Adadnirari III (to 805).

Episodes from Homer's Odyssey were often shown on Greek vases. Here the hero Odysseus drives a stake into the eye of the cyclops, the one-eyed giant, to kill him.

800 Greece: Traditional date for the composition of Homer's epic poems the *Iliad* and the *Odyssey*. (Historians now date them at 700). Mexico: The Olmecs build the earliest American pyramid at La Venta.

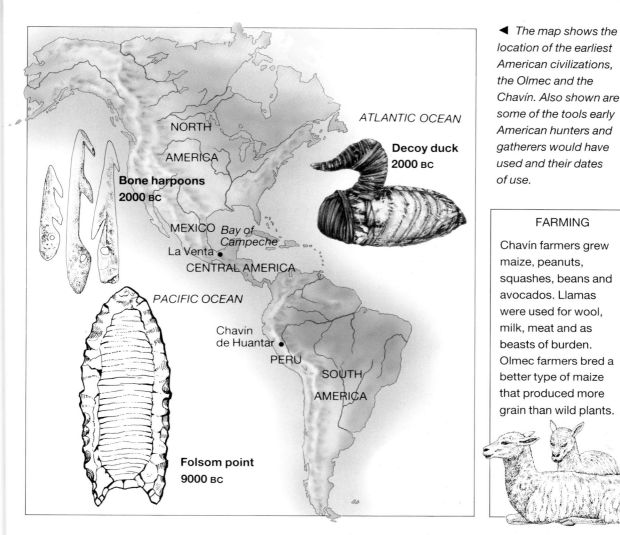

◀ *The map shows the location of the earliest American civilizations, the Olmec and the Chavín. Also shown are some of the tools early American hunters and gatherers would have used and their dates of use.*

NORTH
AMERICA

ATLANTIC OCEAN

Bone harpoons
2000 BC

Decoy duck
2000 BC

MEXICO *Bay of Campeche*
La Venta •
CENTRAL AMERICA

PACIFIC OCEAN

Chavín
de Huantar •
PERU
SOUTH
AMERICA

Folsom point
9000 BC

FARMING

Chavín farmers grew maize, peanuts, squashes, beans and avocados. Llamas were used for wool, milk, meat and as beasts of burden. Olmec farmers bred a better type of maize that produced more grain than wild plants.

◀ *The Olmecs carved enormous stone heads, some of them nearly 3 metres tall. They may represent gods, though the Olmecs worshipped a jaguar god.*

▼ *This fine stone bowl carved in the form of an animal was the work of a Chavín sculptor.*

Olmecs also had a system of writing.

The first permanent settlements in South America were along the coast of northern Peru, where there are traces of fishing and farming communities. About 2800 years ago a more advanced culture appeared, called Chavín after Chavín de Huantar, the site where it was first found. The Chavín people made pottery, wove cloth on looms, built in stone, and made elaborate carvings. The largest building at Chavín de Huantar, the 'castle', is three storeys high. Inside is a maze of rooms, corridors and stairs.

The Chavín culture extended to several other parts of Peru. From their temples and carvings, we know that they worshipped a sacred jaguar or puma.

BC

800–550 India: Aryans expand their territory; gradual development of the caste system.

783–748 Israel: Reign of Jeroboam II: a period of prosperity.

776 Greece: First definitely dated holding of the Olympic games.

770–256 China: Eastern Zhou dynasty.

755 China: Solar eclipse sets the first verified date in Chinese history.

753 Italy: Traditional date of the foundation of Rome by Romulus and Remus; Romulus establishes the first Roman calendar: 10 months with a 60-day break in winter.

c. 750 Africa: An army of the kingdom of Kush defeats the Egyptians at Memphis.

745–727 Assyria: Reign of Tiglathpileser III: huge Assyrian expansion leads to Israel, Damascus, and Babylon paying him tribute.

Leather strips wrapped around the fists were worn by boxers at the first Olympic games.

743 Greece: Sparta begins the First Messenian War to conquer Messenia; it ends in 716.

732 Assyrian armies overthrow the city-state of Damascus.

727 Assyria: Shalmaneser V becomes king (to 722). Two years later he overruns Phoenicia, but is resisted by the Israelites under Hoshea, their 19th and last king.

722–481 China: Period of loose confederations under the Eastern Zhou dynasty.

722 Sargon II of Assyria captures Samaria and brings an end to the kingdom of Israel; 27,000 Israelites reported captive. Egypt: Kushan (Nubian) kings rule over Egypt – the 25th dynasty.

Aryan India

About 3500 years ago a band of pastoralists crossed the mountains of the Hindu Kush into the lands which are now Pakistan and India. They were the Aryans, fleeing from their original homelands in southern Russia. A natural disaster, possibly drought or disease, made them move. They went to Anatolia, to Persia, and finally to India.

The Aryans, whom we also call Indo-Europeans, lived in tribal villages, probably in wooden houses, unlike the brick cities of the Indus Valley people. They counted their wealth in cattle and sheep and were much more primitive than the earlier peoples of the Indian sub-continent. But they were tougher; they were warriors and gamblers, beef eaters and wine drinkers. They loved music, dancing and chariot racing.

Gradually the Aryans settled down and adopted many of the ways of the native Indians, the Dravidians. The Aryans

BUDDHA

Siddhartha Gautama was a prince who lived about 2500 years ago. One day he saw the suffering of ordinary people and abandoned his family to search for a better way of life. He spent his time thinking and preaching. Under a fig tree he achieved enlightenment and became known as the Enlightened One or Buddha. He taught a kinder religion that respected all living creatures. His teachings were popular and before long he had many followers. Buddhism is now one of the world's principal faiths.

CASTE

The Aryans introduced the caste system into India. Society was divided into four classes, or castes. The highest was the Brahman. They were educated priests and scholars and governed the country. The next was the Kshatriya who were soldiers. Third were the Vaisyas who were farmers and merchants. The native Indians of Dravidian origin, whose skin was darker and who were considered inferior, ranked below these three castes and had to serve the upper castes. It was almost impossible to change caste or marry outside it.

Low-caste street trader

High-caste Brahman

SANSKRIT

Sanskrit was the language of the Aryans. The Aryans came from Europe so Sanskrit is related to European languages such as English, German and Latin. It became the language of the Indian upper classes. The first teachings of the Hindu faith, the Vedas, were told in Sanskrit. Most are sacred hymns, but some explain religious rituals. Others are teachings told as a series of questions and answers.

became crop-growers as well as herders. Among the crops was rice, unknown to the Aryans but already grown in the Indus Valley. The use of the plough and the development of irrigation systems enabled the Indo-Europeans to grow more crops, and support larger towns. By 500 BC there were 16 major kingdoms in northern India.

The Aryans had no form of writing. Instead, like the ancient Greeks, they passed on their history and religious beliefs by word of mouth. These traditions, called *Vedas* – Books of Knowledge – were not written down until much later. The oldest is the *Rig-Veda*, a collection of more than 1000 hymns, composed in their language, Sanskrit. The Vedas are the basis of Hinduism, one of the world's oldest religions. Because the Aryans had no written history, most of what we know about their daily lives is from the Vedas. From this we know that an Aryan wife could have many husbands.

▼ *After the Indo-European people, the Aryans, invaded the Indian sub-continent, they dominated the north. Many of the native people, the Dravidians and the Munda, moved into the south and part of east India.*

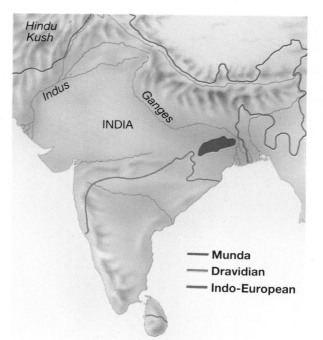

— **Munda**
— **Dravidian**
— **Indo-European**

The Founding of Rome

According to tradition the city of Rome was founded in 753 BC. It was founded by the Etruscans, who chose a strong position on the top of seven hills. At that time, several different peoples lived in Italy. To the south of Rome were the Latini, or Latins.

Legends say that early Rome was ruled by Etruscan kings, of whom Romulus was the first. The citizens were a mixture of Etruscans and Latins, who in time became simply Romans. They were influenced by traders from Greece and

▼ *The Etruscans have left very little writing, but their pictures are vivid. This painting from a tomb shows lyre and flute players entertaining guests at a banquet. The Etruscans were fond of music, games and gambling.*

ROMULUS AND REMUS

According to legend Rome was founded by two brothers, Romulus and Remus. They were the twin grandsons of King Numitor. The king's wicked brother Amulius put the babies in a basket to float down the River Tiber to their deaths. The basket came to land, and the babies were suckled by a she-wolf who had heard the babies' cries. They were raised by a shepherd until one day they were reunited with their grandfather. They founded Rome, but quarrelled and Remus was killed leaving Romulus to become the first king.

SEWERS

Rome had a unique drainage system. It began as a ditch but was later covered by a brick vault. It ran through the whole city and was called the *Cloaca Maxima*. Part of it still exists.

GREEK INFLUENCE

The Etruscans were greatly influenced by the Greeks. They adopted their alphabet, wore togas like the Greeks did and believed in Greek gods. Even the idea of gladiators and games was originally Greek.

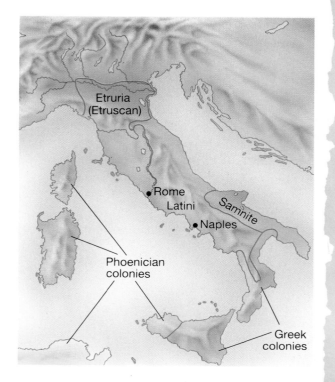

▲ *Italy at the time of the foundation of Rome. The Etruscans came from Etruria. The Greek colonies were along the coast of southern Italy, while the Phoenicians set up colonies in Sicily, Sardinia and Corsica.*

BC
716 Rome: Numa Pompilius becomes the second king of Rome (to 673); he adds January and February to the earlier ten month Roman calendar.

710 The Assyrians destroy the kingdom of Chaldea; Sargon II becomes king of Babylonia.

705 Assyria: Sargon II is killed in battle in Anatolia and he is succeeded by his son Sennacherib (to 682).

701 Assyria: Sennacherib establishes his capital at Nineveh.

700–500 Greece: Formation of the great city-states, such as Athens and Sparta, and the rise of the *hoplites* (foot soldiers).

691–638 Judah: Reign of Manasseh: he encourages the Jews to worship the Assyrian gods.

689 The Babylonians revolt against their Assyrian rulers, who destroy the city and flood the site.

683 Judah surrenders to Assyria; Manasseh becomes a prisoner in Babylon. Greece: City-state of Athens ends the rule of hereditary kings; replaces them with nine *archons* (ministers) chosen each year from among the nobles.

681 Assyria: Sennacherib is assassinated by his elder sons.

680 Assyria: Sennacherib's youngest son, Esarhaddon, succeeds him as king (to 669). Greece: The city-state of Argos becomes powerful under its king, Pheidon.

Carthage, who brought new ideas of culture and government.

The kings of Rome wore togas (cloak-like garments) with purple borders. In processions they were preceded by attendants who carried symbolic bundles of rods, with axes tied to them, called *fasces*. They were a symbol of power and represented the king's right to beat and execute people if they had done wrong. Over two thousand years later they became a symbol of the Fascist party.

Kings did not have complete power. An assembly had a say in who was king and what he could do, especially in war. The kings had armies to defend Rome. Foot soldiers were equipped like the Greeks, with thrusting spears, shields and short swords. Those soldiers who could afford it had body armour with helmets and leg guards.

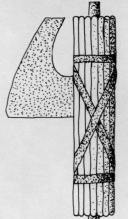

The fasces *was a symbol of power in Rome. The wooden rods symbolized punishment and the axe, life and death.*

War and Weapons

The first people probably fought over food. Their earliest weapons were just rocks and sticks, but later they had spears and arrows tipped with sharpened stones. Once people learned how to make bronze, weapons became more sophisticated. People then fought over riches and territory, but their armies were still just small groups of warriors. The Assyrians were one of the first people to organize a large army. They used cavalry (soldiers on horses) and infantry (foot soldiers), as well as men in chariots. They also had weapons which could demolish the walls built to protect towns. The Greeks also had well organized armies, made up largely of armoured infantrymen, called *hoplites*.

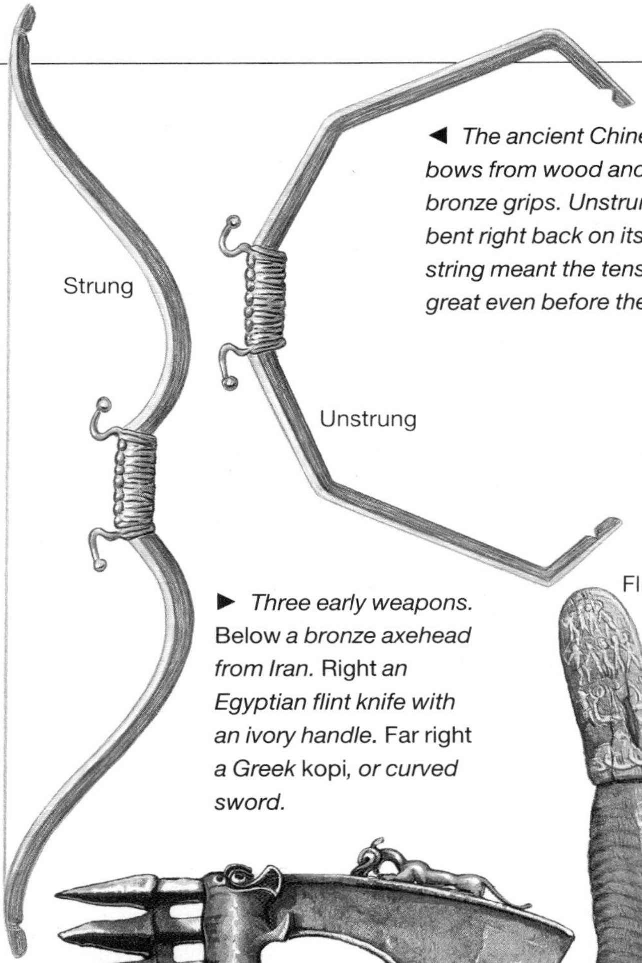

Strung

Unstrung

◀ *The ancient Chinese made bows from wood and bone, with bronze grips. Unstrung the bow bent right back on itself. Adding a string meant the tension was very great even before the archer drew.*

Greek *kopi*

Flint knife

▶ *Three early weapons. Below a bronze axehead from Iran. Right an Egyptian flint knife with an ivory handle. Far right a Greek* kopi, *or curved sword.*

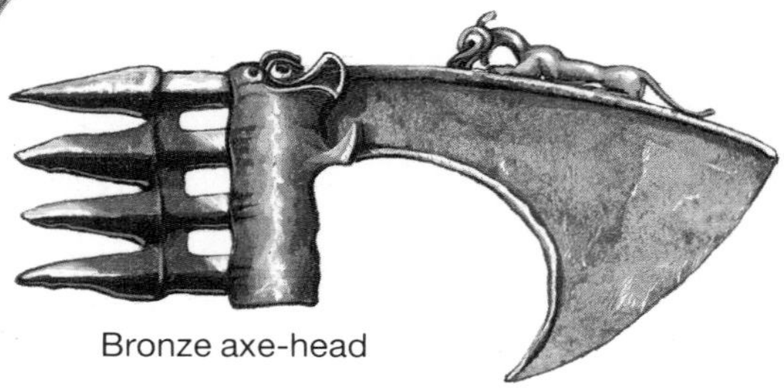

Bronze axe-head

▼ *The Egyptians used fast, two-wheeled chariots in battle. Each chariot had a driver and an archer or a spearman to fight the enemy.*

▼ *The Egyptians fought with bows and arrows and a sickle-shaped sword, called a* khepesh. *They protected themselves with a shield.*

▼ *A Greek cavalryman in battle. His horse is unprotected as it was probably too small to carry his weight, plus that of horse armour.*

WHEN IT HAPPENED

c. **1500 BC** The city of Jericho is attacked by the Israelites and destroyed.

c. **1250 BC** The Greeks capture the city of Troy by a trick. According to legend, a group of Greeks, hidden inside a large wooden horse, get inside the city pretending the horse is a gift. They leave the horse, open the city gates and let their army in to defeat the Trojans.

c. **1122 BC** In China the armies of Wu Wang defeat the armies of the Shang dynasty, bringing the Zhou to power.

689 BC Babylon destroyed by the Assyrians.

671 BC The Assyrians invade Egypt.

► *The Assyrians were experts at siege warfare. Their battering rams could knock holes in town walls, while scaling ladders and towers helped men climb over them. Large shields protected their soldiers.*

BC

680–669 Anatolia: Reign of King Gyges of Lydia, who issues the first datable coins.

669–627 Assyria: Reign of Assurbanipal, the last great king of the country.

664 Egypt: Egypt's governor, Psammetichus, rebels against Assyria and becomes pharaoh, founding the 26th dynasty.

663 Assyria: Army led by Assurbanipal sacks Thebes in Egypt.

660 Byzantium (modern Istanbul) is founded by the Greeks.

652 Babylonia: Shamash-shumuskin, governor for his half-brother, King Assurbanipal, rebels; he kills himself after four years of civil war.

The Persians were among the first people to use bows and arrows in warfare.

650–500 Greece: Period of rule by *tyrants* (self-made dictators) in the city-states.

650 Scythian and Cimmarian raiders sweep over Syria and Palestine. Greece: City-state of Sparta conquers rebellious subjects in the Second Messenian War (to 630).

626 Babylonia: The Chaldean general Nabopolassar seizes the throne and declares Babylonia independent from Assyria.

621 Greece: Athenian minister Dracon provides the city-state with its first written laws, which are severe.

612 Assyria: Medes, Babylonians, and Scythians destroy the capital, Nineveh. End of the Assyrian empire.

608 Pharaoh Necho of Egypt defeats and kills Josiah, king of Judah, at the battle of Megiddo.

605 Babylonia: Reign of Nebuchadnezzar II, the Great (to 561); he defeats Necho and the Egyptians at Carcemish in Syria; Judah comes under Babylonian rule.

Babylon Revived

Tribespeople from the west, called Chaldeans, began migrating into Assyria and Babylonia in about 1100 BC. Several Chaldeans served as kings under their Assyrian overlords. In 626 BC, Nabopolassar declared Babylonia independent and threw off the Assyrian yoke.

Nebuchadnezzar II was one of the most famous kings of Babylonia. He came to power in about 605 BC and his story is told in the Bible, in the book of Daniel. Among other conquests, he captured Jerusalem and forced thousands of its people to live in Babylonia as prisoners.

Nebuchadnezzar also conducted another campaign against Egypt, but devoted most of his time to making the magnificent city of Babylon still more beautiful. He had huge walls built around the city, and named the main gate after the goddess Ishtar. Nebuchadnezzar also built himself a fine

▼ *This map shows the extent of the second Babylonian empire at its height .*

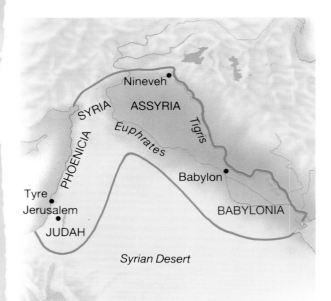

THE HANGING GARDENS

Nebuchadnezzar married a Persian princess, Amytis, who missed the hills of her native land when she moved to the flat plain of Babylon. To please her, Nebuchadnezzar built an artificial 'mountain' in the city. It was made of lofty brick terraces, spread with a thick layer of soil on which flowers and trees were planted. They were irrigated with water carried up from the Euphrates by slaves. Known as the Hanging Gardens of Babylon, the ancient Greeks described them as one of the Seven Wonders of the World.

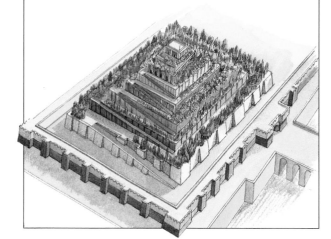

palace and improved other cities in his empire.

The king encouraged the worship of the old Babylonian city god Marduk throughout his empire, which included Syria. In his later years he is believed to have gone mad.

The Babylonian empire survived for only six years after Nebuchadnezzar died. His son, Awil-Marduk ('Evil-Merodach' in the Bible) reigned for three years, before being assassinated. Two other kings, one an infant, reigned for just three more years.

Then a Syrian prince, Nabu-Na'id, seized power, and tried to persuade the people to worship his own god, Sin, rather than Marduk. He made Belsharusur (Belshazzar) co-ruler. In 539 BC Naub-Na'id was deposed and his son killed by the invading Persians under their king, Cyrus II, the Great.

▼ *The annual New Year festival passing through the Ishtar Gate, the northern entrance to Babylon. The gate was covered with blue glazed tiles, decorated with yellow and white figures of bulls and dragons.*

NEBUCHADNEZZAR

Nebuchadnezzar II reigned for 43 years and his reign was marked by many military campaigns. Twice he subdued revolts in Judah and when Phoenicia rebelled he besieged its chief port, Tyre, for 13 years.

Greek Dark Age

When the Mycenaean civilization came to an end in 1100 BC, Greece entered what is called its Dark Age. There is no written history of this period which lasted over 500 years.

The country had been invaded by the Dorians who did not have the culture or the skills of the Mycenaeans; they also spoke a different kind of Greek. However, the invaders did keep alive memories of the Mycenaean age through the tradition of telling long narrative poems. The two greatest of these poems, the *Iliad* and the *Odyssey* by Homer, tell the story of the siege of Troy and the wandering of one of its heroes, Odysseus. Grave goods found in tombs in Mycenae match Homer's descriptions.

Greek warfare developed during the Dark Age. Heavily armed foot soldiers, called *hoplites*, fought in a close formation known as a *phalanx*. In this way they could fight off attacks by fast-moving soldiers on horseback.

▼ When two hoplite phalanxes charged each other it was essential to keep the shield wall unbroken. The end man was most vulnerable because there was no one there to protect him.

WHO WAS HOMER?

According to tradition, Homer was a blind bard who composed the *Iliad* and the *Odyssey* around 800 BC. His fine poetry gives vivid descriptions of people and events. Some scholars think that 'Homer' was several poets who wrote over a long period. More likely he gathered together all the old legends of Mycenae and retold them. Homer would have sung or recited his poems to an audience. The stories may have been written down toward the end of his life.

▲ When invaders overran Greece many of the original inhabitants left to settle elsewhere. The invaders spread out from mainland Greece to settle the islands.

Zhou Dynasty

The Zhou dynasty ruled China for more than 800 years. The Zhou were a group of wandering herders who had settled in the fertile Wei Valley to the west. They ousted the last king of the Shang dynasty, who was cruel and a drunkard. They introduced the working of iron, which they used for weapons and for farm tools such as ploughs. The new metal made farming easier and gave the Zhou soldiers an advantage in war.

The Zhou domain was not a single kingdom, but a collection of large estates, whose owners owed loyalty to the king. Society was divided into the rich nobles, the common people, and slaves. A merchant class also developed.

▲ This picture of an archer mounted on horseback was stamped on a clay tile, made in Zhou times. The bow is similar to those used later in the west.

CONFUCIUS

K'ung Fu-tzu (Great Master Kung), or Confucius, was born in the Zhou period. He taught virtue and responsibility and that everyone had a place in society. His teaching has greatly influenced Chinese thought.

BC

600–480 Growth and expansion of Carthage.

600 Persia (Iran): Windmills are used to grind corn. India: Early cities are set up in the Ganges river valley.

594 Greece: Statesman Solon is made the sole *archon* of Athens; he introduces milder laws to replace those of Dracon, creates a court of citizens and reforms the election of magistrates.

586 Judah: Nebuchadnezzar II of Babylon sacks Jerusalem and takes the people of Judah into captivity in Babylon (the Babylonian Captivity).

580 Babylonia: Nebuchadnezzar II begins building the Hanging Gardens of Babylon, one of the Seven Wonders of the World.

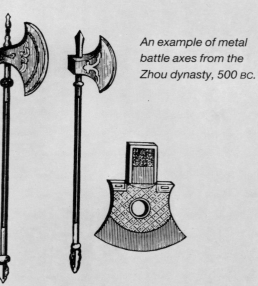

An example of metal battle axes from the Zhou dynasty, 500 BC.

563 India: Birth of Prince Siddhartha Gautama, who later becomes the Buddha (the Enlightened One).

559 Persia: Cyrus II, the Great, becomes king (reigns to 529).

551 China: Birth of the philosopher K'ung Fu-tzu (Great Master Kung, or Confucius).

550 Persia: Cyrus the Great conquers Media and makes it part of the Persian empire.

546 Anatolia: Cyrus the Great of Persia defeats Croesus, last king of Lydia, at the battle of Sardis; the Persians overrun Anatolia.

BC

539 Greeks defeat the Carthaginians in battle. Persia: Cyrus the Great conquers Babylonia.

Mithras, the Persian god of light, shown here killing a bull.

538 End of the Babylonian Captivity: An edict of Cyrus the Great allows some Jewish exiles to return to Judah.

534 Rome: Tarquinius Superbus (Tarquin the Proud), becomes its last king.

530 Persia: Death of Cyrus the Great in battle against Tamyris, Scythian warrior queen and ruler of Massagetae tribe; he leaves an empire that includes Anatolia, Babylonia, Syria and Palestine; succeeded by his son Cambyses (to 521).

525 Egypt is conquered by Cambyses of Persia; the country remains under Persian kings until 404.

521 Persia: Reign of Darius I (to 486); Persian empire is divided into 20 *satrapies* (provinces).

520 Judah: Work is resumed on the Temple in Jerusalem (completed 515).

510 Rome: Rebellion overthrows King Tarquinius Superbus.

509 Rome: Traditional date for the foundation of the Republic.

508 Greece: Statesman Cleisthenes introduces democracy in Athens. Treaty between Rome and Carthage gives Latium to Rome and Africa to Carthage.

507 Greece: City-state of Sparta attempts to restore the aristocracy in Athens.

500 Italy: The Etruscan empire is at its most powerful. India: Start of rice cultivation, writing and coins.

The Persian Empire

The land we call Iran (from the word 'Aryan') used to be known as Persia. Its people were divided into two groups, the Medes and the Persians. They migrated into Persia from the east about 3000 years ago. At first the Medes were more powerful. Nearly 2600 years ago Cyrus, the ruler of the Persian province of Anshan, rebelled against the Medes and seized power.

Cyrus made Persia the centre of a mighty empire, the Persian empire. He became known as Cyrus the Great. His capital was Ecbatana, now buried under the modern city of Hamadan.

Cyrus commanded an army of cavalry and remarkably skilled archers. By the time he died Cyrus ruled over an empire which extended from the Mediterranean Sea to Afghanistan, and from the Arabian Sea north to the Caspian and Aral seas. He was killed in 530 BC defending his northern territories against

DARIUS I

Darius I was a good general, and extended the empire east to the River Indus. He reorganized the empire into 20 provinces called *satrapies*. Good roads allowed the royal messengers to speed to all parts of the land with orders from the king. Darius levied taxes in every part of his empire. He built a new capital city at Persepolis, in southern Iran. He introduced the domestic chicken from India to western Asia, and from Lydia in Anatolia he introduced gold and silver money to Persia. Darius's official title was Shahanshah (king of kings). The title was still in use by the Shah of Iran until the country became a republic in 1979.

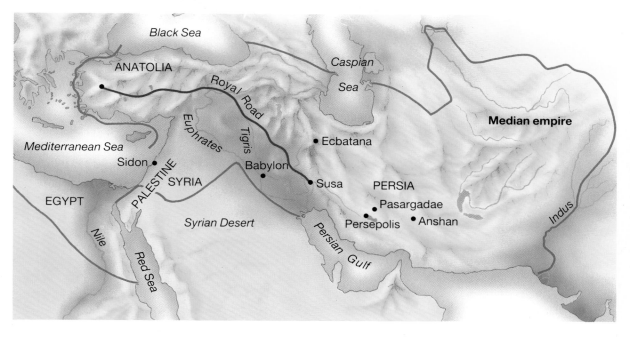

▲ *The Persian empire at its greatest extent under Darius I. Susa was its administrative centre and Persepolis its centre of state. The Royal Road was built to speed up communications.*

▲ *An impression from a cylinder seal shows Darius I hunting a lion from a chariot with bow and arrow. The winged figure is an image of the god Azura Mazda.*

▼ *The steps of the palace at Persepolis show people from all over the empire bringing gifts for the king.*

nomadic tribes from central Asia.

The Persian King Darius I extended and strengthened the empire. He appointed *satraps*, or governors, to each province who paid him gifts of cereals and produce. He built many roads to link his huge empire and encouraged trade by introducing a standard currency.

In religion the Persians followed the teachings of a Persian prophet named Zarathustra (in Greek, Zoroaster), who worshipped the one god Azura Mazda.

Oceania

The first people migrated to Australia from southern Asia. They had to sail across the sea to New Guinea, but the low sea levels left land bridges between New Guinea, Australia and Tasmania. They took with them the dingo, or wild dog. The ancestors of the Aborigines (native Australians) were fishers, hunters and gatherers. They used boomerangs for hunting from very early times and gathered the seeds and fruit of the natural vegetation. The Aborigines never developed farming, but they knew how to use fire to cook their food. As the sea level rose they moved further inland.

The first people to colonize Melanesia and Micronesia sailed from what is now Indonesia about 4000 years ago. Their skilled craft workers built large canoes that could survive long voyages. In the canoes the explorers carried not only supplies for the voyage, but also animals and some of their favourite food plants.

They navigated across the vast distances of the oceans by studying the stars and the sea currents.

▲ *The Aborigines of Australia made paintings, using simple earth colours of red, yellow, brown, black and white. Cave and rock paintings are found in many parts of Australia, some of them at sacred sites.*

▼ *In addition to Australia the map shows the areas of Micronesia (Little Islands) and Melanesia (Dark Islands from the colour of the people) and the approximate date they were settled.*

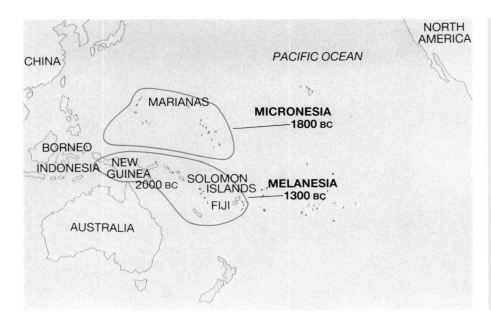

THE DREAMTIME

The Dreamtime is a religious belief that is thousands of years old. It is a creation myth that tells of the Beings that long ago shaped the world and everything in it. The Beings died, but their spirits lived on, some in the sky, others in the ground, in hills, rocks or waterholes. Some Beings are depicted in rock paintings.

Index

This index has been designed to help you find easily the information you are looking for. Page numbers in *italic* type (slanting) refer to pages on which there are illustrations.